RECKONING

PAUL EBERZ

RECKONING

PAUL EBERZ

Cover Design - Paradox Book Cover Designs & Formatting

Line Editor - Carrie Murgittroyd

Printed in the United States of America

First Edition 2021 Copyright 2020 1-10166885971 RECKONING - Paul Eberz

RECKONING – a Just Sugar Production

Ebook ISBN 978-1-7352566-4-1

Paperback ISBN 978-1-7352566-5-8

Hardcover ISBN 978-1-7352566-3-4

Website: BooksbyPaulEberz.

DEDICATION

For Jasen and Zachary. They are the father I always wanted to be.

Illegitimi non carborundum.

ACKNOWLEDGMENTS

The Working Writers Workshop – The Critique Group Extraordinaire. Special thanks; Phil Walker, Diane Dean, Mary Ann Weakley, Shirley Jones.

Beta readers – Joanna Zurn, John Mahony, Patricia Corlett.

Patti Roberts – Paradox Book Covers & Formatting - whose amazing talent made publication a reality.

CONTENTS

Chapter 1 1
Chapter 2 9
Chapter 3 17
Chapter 4 27
Chapter 5 31
Chapter 6 41
Chapter 7 47
Chapter 8 58
Chapter 9 65
Chapter 10 71
Chapter 11 78
Chapter 12 83
Chapter 13 89
Chapter 14 97
Chapter 15 105
Chapter 16 114
Chapter 17 121
Chapter 18 124
Chapter 19 131
Chapter 20 136
Chapter 21 145
Chapter 22 151
Chapter 23 160
Chapter 24 169
Chapter 25 181

Also by Paul Eberz 205
About the Author 207

1

Hamilton Lighter puffed on a Cohiba cigar and exhaled a grey cloud of smoke temporarily obscuring his view of an empty parking lot. He glanced out the driver side window where a single streetlight cast a yellow haze on cracked worn-out asphalt. The boarded-up, red brick warehouse that edged the lot was lifeless, like the sidewalk that surrounded it. He took another puff, then rolled the two-hundred-and-fifty-dollar cigar in his fingers, watching the tip's red glow fade into layered grey ash.

He looked at his watch.

Not midnight

He was parked in an industrial area near the port of Miami. There were no houses, no watchmen, no roving patrols. Just an old lot, with a parked plumber's van, veiled in the shadow of a broken down, abandoned building. Also hidden in plain sight was a black SUV. It was also parked, stationed for its role in the crime.

He removed his phone from his jacket and pressed a number from the recent call's menu. There was an immediate response.

"Yes sir."

"Have the plane ready for takeoff at 3:00 a.m."

"Destination?" replied the pilot.

Hamilton Lighter took a moment to decide. "Milan."

The pilot didn't respond immediately.

"Is there a problem?" Lighter said impatiently.

"No, sir. I'll call the FAA and the ENCA for clearance."

"Remind me what the ENCA is again?"

"The Italian version of our Federal Aviation Administration. I need to file a flight plan for the points of departure and arrival. I would suggest Milan Liate Airport as the destination. It's about five miles east of Milan and specializes in private air travel. It suits your travel plans better than either Milan Malpensa or Orio airports."

"Time of arrival?"

There was another pause. "It will be approximately fourteen hours including a one-hour refueling stop at Blackbushe airport in England. A departure at 3 a.m. EST puts arrival at Milan Liate about noon tomorrow." The pilot seemed confidant with his calculation.

Hamilton didn't respond.

"Sir... is there anything else?"

"Do you file flight plans with Interpol?"

"I don't but I would assume the airports are required to do so."

Lighter smiled and pushed disconnect, the phone's glowing light the only illumination. He leaned back in the driver seat of the van and picked up the S.T. Dupont Ligne Champagne cigar lighter from the console. His fingers caressed the diamond encrusted gold lighter, then flipped the lid, igniting its carefully engineered blend of yellow and blue flame. For a second, he remembered it cost $79,000 dollars—a half a second.

A muffled moan disturbed the enjoyment of this extravagance.

He pressed the recent icon on the phone and touched the second number.

Angela Bower, his personal assistant, answered on the first ring. "Sir."

"I need a car at Milan Liate Airport at noon tomorrow."

"Type?"

"A Mercedes-S or Citroen DS. Make sure the driver knows Milan very well...fluent English and Italian."

"Of course. Hotel?"

"What do you recommend?"

"Either the Bulgari or the Palazzo. Both are five-star and the best of the best in Milan."

"You pick. Tell the driver."

"How long?"

"Six days."

"Entertainment after you arrive?"

"Hmmm. I'll decide on the rest of my stay later but tomorrow night, after eleven... a nightclub."

"Yes, sir. I suggest Gattopardo, it's a popular disco. Afterhours, I recommend Capriccio Club Prive'. Will you require an escort?"

"Yes."

"Preference— nationality, hair, type?"

"Ah...Italian—I want a translator. Dark hair... worn up and no perfume."

"Choice of type; Cinderella, disco queen, sophisticate, slut?"

"Surprise me."

"Just one?"

"Yes, I'll find another at the disco but... ahhh... on second thought, have another at the disco in case I'm not inspired by the local talent."

"Yes, sir."

He disconnected.

The smell of urine made him wince and spin around in the seat. He hit the flashlight function on his phone and shone into the rear compartment.

She lay amidst lengths of plastic pipe, construction debris, and an assortment of plumbing tools. Her eyes darted back and forth, her head bobbing up and down, struggling helplessly on the cold metal floor. Her yoga pants were stained and a yellow puddle was on the floor. What wasn't hidden behind the duct tape covering her mouth was contorted in fear.

Her hands and her feet, nails painted with bright red

polish, were secured with plastic ties. Everything was taped or tied except for her eyes. What she could see was irrelevant.

Hamilton Lighter stubbed out the cigar and put the lighter in the pocket of the average-man sweatshirt. Later, before he boarded the plane, he would be wearing the clothes protected by a garment bag hanging behind him on a hook meant for extension cords.

On the floor next to the woman was a duffle bag, custom made with spun bound, nonwoven, dissolving fabric. The work clothes he had on would go into the duffle bag, along with his shoes, his underwear—and the woman on the floor.

A box of white latex gloves sat on the console. They went on easily. He didn't need to be careful about fingerprints or DNA in the truck. His attention needed to be only on what he would put inside the envelope laying on the dashboard. After snapping the gloves at the wrist, he picked it up and read the address.

Federal Bureau of Investigation
26 Federal Plaza – 23rd floor
New York, New York.
Attn: Behavioral Analysis Unit 5.

On the inside of the flap there were block letters.

Taken – September 23
Expired – Midnight – September 25.

Even through the plastic gloves he could feel the weight of the paper. It was heavy and expensive. He had stolen it from a stationary store in Zurich. He grinned, knowing it would distract his trackers for days. He placed it inside the pouch of his sweatshirt.

He checked his watch, 11:54.

Showtime.

The door handle of the old van needed an extra jerk. Stepping out, he sucked in a deep breath of night air and gave the street one final look before sliding the side panel open. The squeaky hinges broke the silence. Even in the dim light, he could see her wide blue eyes, pupils dilated with fear, and tears flowing down her cheeks. She was sucking air though her nose and the duct tape over her mouth was pulsing in and out. Every muscle of her body looked stretched to its breaking point.

Lighter leaned over, getting close to her face, stopping when he smelled her fear. For a moment he wanted to whisper her name but he couldn't remember it. His finger pulled a length of hair away from her face. It was wet with sweat. He twirled it around his finger and stretched it out. It was blond. He ran it under his nose. There was a faint scent of some kind of girly soap. He pulled back a couple of inches, looked her in the eyes then yanked the hair from her head.

To his disappointment there was almost no reaction.

I'll bet you'll feel this.

The plastic chamber of the long needle he had in his hand was wide and filled with an amber-colored fluid. His nose was an inch away from hers when its point pieced her neck. He pushed the plunger and a lethal dose of pure nicotine, *nicotinana tabacum*, flowed into her bloodstream.

She went stiff, her breathing rapid.

The moaning stopped when her blue eyes became grey.

Lighter pushed himself up to a sitting position and removed the envelope from his sweatshirt. He lifted the flap, put in the hair, then ran the adhesive over the hole left by the needle. A tiny drop of blood oozed onto the paper. He took the edge and smeared it over the sweat on her face, sealed the letter, and put it back in his sweatshirt.

He looked at her and shrugged at the effort he needed to put into his next task. As he backed out of the van he pulled on the feet with the painted toenails. He yanked until the body thumped when it hit the asphalt. He grabbed and unzipped the duffle bag. It only took about two minutes to stuff the body into the bag. He had a lot of practice and knew exactly how to bend her to fit. When finished, he stepped back and admired his handiwork. Standing in the empty parking lot, he stripped naked, except for the rubber gloves, then carefully laid the old clothes on top of the body. He checked the ground to make sure he hadn't dropped anything then reached inside the van and removed the garment bag from the hook. Inside was a complete change of clothes including a Luigi Borrelli shirt, an Amani suit, and Testoni shoes. When he finished adjusting the Dior tie, he took the envelope from the sweatshirt and placed it inside the jacket.

He closed the door on the van and extended the handle on the duffel. The wheels on the bag bounced on loose stones as he dragged it to the black SUV parked behind the van. The weight of the bag was well under his dead lift capacity, lifting it into the trunk wasn't hard.

Returning to the van, he popped the door on the gas tank and stuffed two feet of cloth down the fill tube, leaving a portion hanging out. The blue flame from the solid gold lighter emitted a small yellow glow on the end of the cloth.

The SUV started quietly and the only noise that could be heard was from the stones that shot out from under the tires as it accelerated. Lighter turned out of the parking lot just as the van exploded. Through the rearview mirror, he saw the vehicle lift off the asphalt, twist in mid-air, then fall back to ground on its side, engulfed in flames.

2

The quiet click of the limo door closing was vastly different than the trash-can bang of his van door. Smoke hadn't been in his vehicle for almost a year. It was idle and gathering bird shit, parked behind his two-room, walk-up apartment in Northeast Philadelphia. He had taken up residence in a posh, SoHo luxury condo but the sound emanating from the finely engineered, black-glass vehicle always reminded him from whence he came.

He settled into the seat behind the driver and turned to Dr. Olivia Bennet. "You sure you're ready for this?"

She smiled, that smile, and didn't answer.

Smoke didn't smile back. "You know, it's not what he says it is?"

She winced. "I agreed with you the first time you said that, and the three times you repeated it, and now again... I know, it's not what he says it is."

"I didn't mean to say you didn't. I guess what I actually mean is, your old boss, the head of the forensic investigation unit of the FBI, suddenly calls you, out of the blue, and insists he needs you to speak to a bunch of recruits. It doesn't ring true."

"Actually, he didn't say recruits. He said agents."

Smoke was a little surprised she hadn't corrected that before, but decided to let it pass. "Okay, agents. But you agree then, this is probably about a case. And with that in mind, need I remind you; it's only been three months since you were... shot in the head. Don't you think it's a little too soon for you to get involved in a criminal case?"

"First, I am willing to assume it's a speech and not a case and, second, I wasn't shot in the head, my forehead was nicked by a bullet. I had stiches and a headache. You... however, were shot twice, went into a coma, and almost died. So, the question is not should I be going, but should you?"

He dropped his hands to his lap, hating that he had no comeback.

She reached across the vast expanse of the backseat and took his hand. She stared with loving determination and didn't speak.

He was used to seeing her self-assured attitude, her brashness—sometimes even the look of street-tough impudence but he saw something different this time. Her expression wasn't locked in, it was softer, accepting. Her head tilted a bit and her chin was up to what he thought was resolve of some inner conflict. There was a glint of resignation in her eyes, an unavoidable submission to something out of her control.

She reacted to his wordless insight. A short, uncontrolled sigh made her suddenly turn away.

He squeezed her hand. "I told you... I will never let anybody hurt you, again."

She turned back to him. A tear was rolling down her cheek.

His big hand gently wiped it away.

They were driving from SoHo to Midtown Manhattan to see someone Dr. Olivia Bennet hadn't seen in eight years, her former boss, the head of a division of the FBI. He recruited her as a senior at the University of Virginia. She accepted an internship. He wanted her to join up right after she graduated. But she wanted her Doctorate. So, she made him wait. After graduating summa cum laude from UV, she went to the Sorbonne in Paris for her Masters, returned to the U.S. for her PsyD in Forensic Psychiatry at Stanford. Although it was years later, she still wanted the position with the FBI. Her choice was etched in stone by a deep unhealable wound —the murder of her sister.

The limo driver took Broadway to Canal Street, then Lafayette south, moving quickly past the Art Deco, Beaux Art, Postmodern, and Italianate style buildings. Icons of architectural elegance appeared like exhibits in a living museum. Their destination was a structure that would not have been a curator's selection. The Jacob K. Javits Federal Building that housed the New York division of the FBI didn't belong to one of the architectural design categories. There were no architectural lines of artistry, no granite edifices, or bronze statues of dead men. Dull-brown, concrete strips stacked floor upon floor were interrupted with narrow, black, equally-spaced, windows causing the building to resemble a multi-tiered jail. However visually disturbing the design, it did accurately reflect the attitude of the people who worked there—cold, hard, and totally without frills.

The Federal Bureau of Investigation has four divisions; Cybercrime, Counter Terrorism, Counter Intelligence, and Criminal Investigation that operate in fifty-six division offices across the US and Puerto Rico. In support of the Criminal Investigation Division is the National Center of Analysis of Violent Crime, located in Quantico, Virginia. The key division in the Center is Behavioral Analysis, Unit-5 or BAU-5. Its mission is to understand the criminal psyche, who criminals are and how they think. The unit develops research and reviews evidence, in conjunction with ongoing state and federal investigations, but also works independently, diligently searching the darkest corners for society's deadliest demons.

BAU-5 also has the highest turnover of personnel. The day-to-day horror show often proves impossible for some, but the ones who overcome revulsion and can control anxiety and stress are amongst the most dedicated and talented professionals in law enforcement.

Dr. Oliva Bennet and Henry "Smoke" Smokehouse

entered the main floor of 26 Federal Plaza and were seated on an uncomfortable metal and plastic couch near the reception desk. While Olivia reviewed her notes, Smoke examined the starkly decorated area. There were no magazines or newspapers and the only things on the walls were a picture of Donald Trump above a plaque that read *President of the United States*. Next to it was a blank space where a picture should be hanging over a plaque that read *Director of the FBI*. Smoke wasn't up on current events but figured a leadership transition was ongoing.

"Dr. Olivia Bennet. Oh my God, it's so good to see you." A short, grey-haired man in a dusty cardigan sweater came out of an elevator with stretched out arms, apparently looking for a hug.

"George, you look exactly the same as the last time I saw you." Dr. Bennet put her arms around him.

Her embrace humored Smoke. She was a good five inches taller than the man and the hug was, his head to her chest, rather than his cheek to her cheek.

Still smiling, she held out her hand to Smoke. "George DiSanto, let me introduce you to—."

"Mr. Henry Smokehouse." George turned to Smoke with a toothy grin peeking out from under his beard and moustache. "I believe Smoke is preferred... native of Philadelphia. Great references from local Philadelphia and New York PD. Enlisted in the Army after LaSalle University, two tours, Iraq and Afghanistan, multiple commendations, including two purple hearts and..." his tone changed from resume to respect, "the Distinguished Service Cross for above and beyond."

Smoke was stone-faced and silent.

Her shoulders pushed back with pride.

"But," George extended his hand, "More important than all of that, you sir, have won the heart of this woman." George held on to Smoke's hand and took hers, "and that's no small accomplishment."

She blushed.

Smoke did not.

"Come on, I have a pot of fresh coffee waiting, and the chairs in the office I'm using weren't purchased from Dungeons R Us."

On the 24th floor, they walked to a key-coded, steel door and into an office bullpen of desks occupied by men and women, all dressed in dark colored jackets and white shirts. Smoke noticed that a few of the younger suits dared to wear multicolored ties. They all had shiny shoes.

Dr. Bennet, looking like the sun at midnight, had chosen a red business suit. Smoke had dug up a well-seasoned corduroy jacket, which he wore over newish blue jeans and a black t-shirt. He and Olivia seemed out of place but so did Cardigan George.

The black and whites glanced at the strangers as they passed, but didn't stare.

"Here we are." George pointed to an open door, and gestured them inside. "Come on in, have a seat."

The office was decorated in early trash dump. Stacks of paper were teetering on overtaxed shelves, on the conference table, and piled in several thigh-high stacks on the floor. Smoke thought a loud voice might cause an avalanche.

"I was so happy you accepted my invitation to speak to our agents, Olivia."

"How could I say no after you went to all the trouble arranging this soiree here in New York instead of at Quantico. When we worked together in Virginia, you hardly ever left the building, not even to go home to change clothes. George, seriously, it's time for a new sweater."

"Never, I just got this broken in." He smiled. "But really it was no trouble and I have to admit, Oliv...wait." A sardonic grin appeared. "Should I be calling you Dr O?"

She waved her hand, a little red in her cheeks. "I haven't talked to you since my book was published, have I?"

"Nope."

"I got pegged with that nickname by the press after my book was published. My choice of subject matter was titillating, and the press dubbed me Dr. Orgasm which was shortened to Dr. O." Her voice became reverent. "I would like it if you called me Olivia. It makes me feel like I'm your intern again."

He winked. "Olivia, it is, then." He looked at a clock on the wall. "We should go. Your audience is a dozen staff from Quantico and thirty agents from offices in Albuquerque, Boston, Philadelphia, Norfolk, Charleston, Little Rock, Las Vegas, Tulsa, Dallas, Los Angeles, Chicago, Denver, Phoenix, and Honolulu."

"Really?" She seemed surprised. "Tell me, they're not all here just for my lecture?"

There was a pregnant pause before George answered. "No... no, of course not."

Smoke said his first words. "Seems like pretty specific offices for a lecture entitled 'Adopting Multi-Disciplinary Perspectives for Serial Murder Investigations'."

For an instant George seemed to have forgotten Smoke was in the room. He pushed his chair back and stood quickly. "Ah...yes, I guess it is, pretty specific. Shall we go?"

George came around the desk, took her by the arm, and led her to the door where Olivia walked out first. George followed and as he did, turned and looked at Smoke.

Smoke said softly, "Pretty specific offices."

George paused a second then nodded.

Smoke nodded back. They both understood this was about more than just a speech.

3

A PowerPoint slide was displayed on a white board and a single spotlight illuminated the podium where Dr. Bennet stood. A microphone amplified her soft voice to a volume that commanded audience attention. FBI agents, sitting in elevated auditorium seats, were riveted to her detailed and complicated lecture.

Smoke sat alone, up in the last row. His butt was sore and he needed to stretch but he remained in his chair, observing the audience. Part of the group appeared to be partners. Fifteen pairs of agents occasionally whispered comments and looked at each other's notes. Twelve agents, he assumed were from Quantico, sat six in a row and six in the row behind, each taking notes and none of them talking.

He found it difficult to follow all of the data, occasionally getting lost when medical terms became the foundation of the presentation. It wasn't all bad. When she converted the med-

speak to street-speak, he caught up. However, the dark room, uncomfortable seats, and hard focused attention were taking a toll and yawns were getting harder to suppress. Finally, he recognized his Sherlock Holmes-like deductive reasoning was working at one hundred percent efficiency when he construed she was near the end of her presentation because the slide on the wall screen read, Conclusion.

Unlike Smoke, she looked as fresh as when she had begun her speech. She clicked the button on a remote and the screen went back to the first slide.

Adopting Multi-Disciplinary Perspectives for Serial Murder Investigations
Doctor Olivia Bennet

Clinical Psychologist. Forensic Psychologist, Author
Md, PhD, PsyD.
University of Virginia, Paris-Sorbonne University, Stanford University
Federal Bureau of Investigation, BA-Unit 5
Consulting Forensic Psychologist New York State Police

She pointed to the slide. "There's a lot of letters up there indicating I know what I'm talking about...clinically. But the truth is, there's a lot of people, equally, if not better qualified than I, who could deliver this same speech. What I have said today is not new. It is merely a collection of facts, terms, and deductions, documented by qualified men and women who have spent years dissecting this type of individual. To be effective in your job— the vocation you have decided to pursue— you...need...to know this shit forward and backwards."

A little laughter came up.

Her attitude changed from giving an informational classroom lecture to a football half-time mandate. "Your boss, George DeSanto, could have ten other experts give this speech but he chose me, someone who left BAU-5 seven years ago." She took the mic from its stand and walked to the edge of the podium platform. "He chose me because I am an expert in this field... and he chose me because I am, also, a victim."

No pins dropped.

"What I am about to say is the most important thing you will hear today." She raised her hand and pointed at the group. "The people you investigate are the single-most dangerous threat to the lives of the public that you will encounter in your career. You are pursuing schizophrenic serial murderers who are brutally violent, and incapable of remorse or pity. They are calculating and structured, but when cornered, they are unpredictable. To them everything is a game of deception. They bask in the thrill of the hunt, the kill and eluding capture. They hide in plain sight, assuming average, every day, occupations while their secret-selves, their alter egos, plan their next crime. They believe they are superior beings, gifted and unique."

She walked back to the podium and into the spotlight. "Some are caught due to the tireless efforts of law enforcement. Some, like Bundy, because of a broken taillight.

But all of them have one constant— the need for attention... which is why so many make contact with the media. These monsters...need to kill like you need to breathe."

She switched hands with the microphone, moving it close to her mouth. "This unit... the BAU, works to find one flaw, a singular miscalculation, the one mistake that will chase them out from the shadows, into the light. However, you must remember while they are not only a deadly threat to their victims, they are also a very, real threat to you. At the same time, you are looking for them...they are watching you."

"You are an integral part of their fantasy, and as important to their delusion as their victims." She looked into the audience. "Someday, you may find yourself with your guns drawn and a dark hallway between you and the suspect. If, in that moment, you think you have the advantage... you will be wrong. If you think your presence wasn't anticipated, you will not realize the dark hallway in front of you is a trap. So, don't be arrogant or overconfident. You must always anticipate the unexpected."

Every face was leaning forward.

She stopped, looked around the room, then in a loud voice bellowed. "Did I get your attention?"

Two weak "yes's" came from the group.

"Did you hear me?" Her voice bounced off the back wall.

A loud response erupted. "Yes."

"Good, now go catch these... sons of bitches."

Applause rose, as did the audience.

George DiSanto, applauding, walked toward her. "Brilliant." He kissed her cheek. "You still got it."

Smoke came down from the cheap seats and strolled across the aisle toward them.

George whispered to Olivia, "Your man walks like a western movie star."

"Philly swagger," she whispered back.

George looked up from his five foot five to Smoke's six foot two. "There is something else I would like to show both of you."

O and Smoke looked at each other with a 'there it is' look.

The three walked down a long corridor to double grey steel doors.

George hesitated before pushing the handle down. "I want your impressions about what you are about to see. I want your observations of what you see, cold, with no explanations. Okay?"

Olivia stepped forward nodding. "Of course, no pro—"

"No, no, not yours," George gazed up at Smoke. "I want to hear what you have to say about what's behind these doors."

Smoke shrugged.

They were alone in a long, narrow room. Desks, backed one against another, formed a row down the middle. Smoke presumed the desk at the far end of the row belonged to George, because of the piles of paper appearing to be ready to topple over.

Smoke stepped forward, leaving Olivia and George at the door, his attention drawn to the walls on either side of the room. There were long white boards attached to the two side-walls. Each board was equally sectioned with red tape, ten divisions on the right and ten on the left. All of the sections on the right had photographs, newspaper clippings, police reports, and maps displayed, top to bottom. The exhibits had black ink labels and color-coded pins with red string connecting one to another. Five sections on the left wall had the same displays, with photos, pins and the red string. Five sections were empty.

Smoke started on the right, reading, moving slowly, stopping to examine the small print on a police report, or a caption on a photo, taking almost a half hour to get to the last section. When finished, he walked with his head down, across the back of the room, past George's desk to the board on the other side of the room. Beginning again, he examined every piece of paper.

When he finished the last of the exhibits, he walked past the five blank sections, but stopped before reaching Olivia and George. He looked toward them but not at them.

They were watching him work the problem.

A new thought came to him, followed by quick steps back to the last section he examined, where a police report and a photo were scrutinized. A finger went to his lips, then tapped his head. Stepping back, head lowered, he began pacing back and forth in front of the empty sections.

Olivia nudged George. "He thinks better when he moves."

Smoke stopped, looked across the room and returned to the first section of evidence. Again, two documents were examined closely.

He raised a finger into the air.

"He's close," she said, smiling.

He almost trotted back across the room to the last section. He ran his finger over one exhibit, tapped it, and walked deliberately toward the waiting pair.

Smoke arrived in front of George. "Why haven't you put up the last investigation? Number 16 is missing?"

A slight grin appeared on George's face and he tapped his chin with his forefinger. "A few people I respect told me you were good... but I had to see it for myself."

Smoke caught her eye and motioned a sweeping gesture around the room. "The FBI is actively investigating the kidnapping and murder of fifteen...no, sixteen young women." He turned to the BAU section chief. "George thinks all of them are linked and somehow are a direct threat to you."

She let out a slight gasp. "What? George, is he right?"

George took her elbow and walked her toward the walls of evidence. "Yes, Smoke is right. Obviously, I need to explain."

She responded with attitude. "Obviously."

"Each one of these sections has information pertaining to a case that has very few common elements. The victims are women, between 21 and 22 years old, long brown hair, and brown eyes. They are fit, about five seven and approximately 125 pounds. Each disappeared without a trace leaving no crime scenes, no forensics, and no bodies to be found. There have been no ransom notes, and no contact of any kind with any family or the local PD. And... that is where the similarities end." His hand swept across the room. "They are difference races, come from different cities, and had different occupations. Some were married, some single, six were college students, two were nurses and there were two waitresses. There was a grad student, a lawyer, and a prostitute." He walked up to the first section and pointed to an envelope. "About a week after each disappearance, the FBI division office, nearest to where the victim was abducted, received an envelope by mail. Inside was a lock of hair and a smudge of blood identifying the victim. Inside the killer wrote this."

He lifted the flap of the envelope in the first section. It read: Taken - June 23. Expired -Midnight - June 25.

"This was his first."

George studied Smoke. "Before I go any further, what else did you see?"

Smoke looked at him a bit defiant, resenting being tested.

She took his elbow and nodded him on.

"Okay if I must. Everything placed on the boards is less than a week old. Every photograph, map, report, and every mark used to draw a line or a notation is fresh. The first Missing Person Report is dated sixteen months ago, June 23, 2019. The last one, number 15," he said pointing to the last section of exhibits. "is dated August 25, 2020, one month ago."

"What does that tell you?" George prodded.

"First you just convened this investigation and today is October 11 and you haven't posted a September 25 murder."

"You're right, we have just made the connection, and we

haven't posted the last victim's information. So, what does that mean?"

"It means you didn't post the September missing person report because it was different than the others and that variance is the connection and the reason we're here."

George seemed impressed.

"And..." Smoke wasn't done. "There was another body associated with the September kidnapping and murder."

George's mouth dropped open. "How—?"

"The exhibits were up, but you had them taken down. There are tape marks and pin holes in the wall."

"How did you deduce the other body?"

"There is residue on the wall from the outlines where pictures of two different people were posted." Smoke stopped and stared at George. "The missing person is a woman like the others, 21, brown hair, 122 pounds. She went missing and there is no body. The other picture you took down was of the body of a man."

George smiled a professorial smile "Now, I'm impressed. You are correct, but how did you know it was a man?"

"I didn't. I had a fifty-fifty shot and you confirmed it. Now, I get to ask a question."

George nodded. "Okay?"

"How is this connected to O?"

George turned to Olivia. "You already know, don't you?"

She nodded and a whisper from her past crept out. "There is another common element, isn't there?"

George didn't answer.

She looked up at Smoke. "They all had twin sisters."

She buried her head in Smoke's chest. "It's him."

George looked at Smoke. "Yes, I'm afraid it is. We believe the man responsible for this mayhem is the man who killed your twin sister—Hamilton Lighter."

Smoke heard a moan come up from her soul.

"Olivia." George's voice was firm and demanding.

Her head turned to him.

"We need your help to catch him."

4

Three Pratt and Whitney engines provided the power to drive one hundred feet of aviation perfection at the land speed of 450 per hour. It was under its top end but Hamilton was on a predetermined schedule and distance and time was a calculation not a race. The Falcon 7x floated in the stratosphere appearing almost motionless against the stars.

"LGN4375, this is Air Traffic Control New York, Over."

"Air Traffic New York, this is LGN4375. Go Ahead."

"LGN4375 acknowledge you are leaving Air Traffic Control, New York on your flight plan."

"Acknowledge, New York LGN4375 is leaving your control and switching to International Air Traffic Control in Swanwick, Hampshire, England."

"Roger your transmission, LGN4375. Good night and God speed."

There was a communications gap between the two air control authorities. It would be a few minutes before someone watching a screen in England would notice that an aircraft in the middle of the Atlantic Ocean was a little late in making contact. The tactic had worked sixteen times before without raising an alert.

Captain Harry Geller hit the plane's cabin intercom alerting its passenger to be ready. "Our descent will begin in sixty seconds."

First Officer Chad Watson reached to the control panel above his head and began his checklist, preparing for the unauthorized descent.

The Captain knew that varying a flight plan without cause was a major infraction of FAA regulations. If investigated, they would claim an emergency loss of cabin pressure forced the action he and his co-pilot were about to initiate. The pilot was quite willing to follow the direction of his employer because he needed the job. Three DUIs had made him virtually unemployable as a commercial pilot, which was unfortunate because Geller was more than good, he was an excellent pilot. Having qualified as a Navy top-gun flyer, he commanded F-16s in fifty sorties in Afghanistan. However, his transition to civilian life proved more taxing than he anticipated. He flew 747s for United, but abuse of drugs and alcohol ended his career when he put his SUV through a supermarket window at three in the morning.

Cory Watson's problem was less impactful on real-estate, but equally as damaging to his career. Although his issues were not a result of military service, he did have problems with substance abuse and that manifested when he arrived to crew a flight too high on opioids to remember his shoes.

Mr. Lighter, then a resident of Central State Hospital for the Criminally Insane in Petersburg, Virginia, had contacted Geller. In that very odd telephone call, Lighter acknowledged Geller's flying ability and the raw deal he had received from his employer. He offered the pilot a five-year contract at triple what he was making at United. Lighter also told him, if he accepted, his attorneys would clear the way for a quick re-instatement of his pilot's license. Mr. Lighter said Cory Watson already accepted a co-pilot contract and together they would be flying a brand new, highly customized Falcon 7x.

There were two other people in the flight crew, both worked the cabin. Kathy Ferguson and Joan Pitcher also had issues but were now loyal to Lighter's money and they also knew what was about to happen. Anticipating the maneuver, they stowed all equipment and cleared the galley.

Geller checked his watch and reached for the cabin mic. "Beginning maneuver."

He calculated he had fifteen minutes to return to this elevation. He set the controls above his head and on the instrument panel, then pushed the yoke forward. The jet's, nose dropped and the plane began a rapid descent. It accelerated to 550 MPH. At 30,000 feet, he leveled off, reduced speed, and checked the gauge indicating the pressure in the hold was equalized with the pressure outside. Opening the belly ramp too soon would mean a sudden end to the flight.

He hit the intercom. "In position."

Hamilton Lighter took another sip of bourbon, and placed his glass in a cup holder. He then flipped open the top of the arm rest, revealing a small control panel inside. Two toggle switches marked OPEN and CLOSE were located between two LED lights, one of which had just turned green. He put his finger on the toggle marked OPEN and pressed it down. The LED light began flashing red. The sound of hydraulics filled the cabin, followed by a thump as something metal locked into place under the belly of the plane. The plane emitted a shudder. It shook then vibrated. A monitor anchored to the cabin wall had the view from the camera in the cargo hold on the screen. The payload placed in the middle of the ramp began to move, sliding slowly at first then quickly toward the opening. Hamilton watched, then smiled as he pressed the toggle marked CLOSE.

As soon as the ramp winding motor stopped, Lighter was pushed back into his seat as the engines powered up, lifting the plane back to 50,000. He flipped the lid closed on the control panel to the very expensive, very custom feature.

Lighter looked out the porthole. It was a beautiful night, clear, almost cloudless. The water below, glistening in the moonlight, reached out to where the horizon ended and the stars began. Nothing disturbed the ocean below except the momentary splash of a body in a duffle bag.

5

George led Smoke and Doctor Bennet to a small table and chairs outside his avalanche of an office. No one had spoken since leaving the evidence room. A plate of sandwiches from a local deli and a pot of coffee had been placed in anticipation of their arrival.

Smoke poured a cup for himself and for Olivia.

George studied their faces. "You knew this was about him before you arrived or at least you suspected, yes?"

She nodded but remained silent.

"You know everything?" George engaged Smoke.

Smoke reflected on the question before responding. "I think you need to understand my role. I came to New York to help out on a different issue which was complicated—"

George held up a stop sign. "No need to go through the details. I was briefed by your contact in the Philadelphia Police Department, Lieutenant Robert Aimer, and I'm certain what happened then, why you came to New York, is unrelated."

Olivia had her head down and spoke quietly. "I didn't tell Smoke about Lighter until three months ago which was after Smoke and I... let's just say my trust for this man developed over time."

George nodded.

"I got a call from Dr. Black at Central State Hospital more than a year ago. I was told that Hamilton Lighter was going to be released."

Smoke covered her hand with his. "I knew there was a threat but Lighter wasn't on my radar." Smoke took a sip of coffee before continuing. "Before I accepted the protection job, before I met Olivia, I did a threat assessment recon outside her office. I took a lot of pictures. Months later, after she told me about him, I went back and looked at those photos again. I found two pictures of Lighter in the crowd, outside her office."

"Nothing since then?"

He shook his head. "No."

She put her hands flat on the table. "George, I heard it in your voice when you asked me to do this talk. Now, after what you showed us in there..." she shook her head and whispered, "My God, sixteen girls."

George seemed determined to move forward. "If you don't object, Olivia, I would like to brief Smoke on our background. Okay?"

She nodded.

"As a part of my responsibilities as head of this

department, I stay in touch with Psychology Departments at several universities looking for gifted students to recruit for the FBI. Olivia was recommended while she was completing her last year of undergraduate work at the University of Virginia. Her talent for profiling proved to be extraordinary and I invited her to intern for the FBI at Quantico, as a part of her course work during her senior year."

George got up, walked the few steps into his office. Amongst the piles he immediately found a single file which he placed on the table in front of Smoke. "Over the years, the BAU-5 has interviewed incarcerated serial murderers. We then developed comparison trait analysis programs to find similarities amongst all murderers nationwide. These programs are a work in progress and constantly updated. Olivia was assigned to a team reviewing a program detailing similarities in the abduction and murder of young women."

Olivia gazed up at Smoke. "I have resisted telling you the whole story. I didn't want to be afraid so I denied he was a threat. I knew he was out but, since there was no contact, I..."

"I understand. It's okay."

She took a breath and began. "It all began during my junior year. I met Lighter, or rather he met me, when he 'accidently' knocked me down in a crowded hallway. He apologized and insisted on buying me dinner. He was funny, charming, handsome... and disarming. We dated a few times, three times to be accurate, and they were all completely social. Very friendly but not intimate. I was busy with my studies and didn't think much of it or him. When the term ended, I went home for summer break but when I returned in the fall, I found him waiting outside my dorm. I was surprised and a little flattered. After that I found myself agreeing to several more dates."

She reached over and took the file from George, leaving it unopened in front of her. "He was fascinated by psychology and what I was studying. When I told him about interning with the BAU he wanted to know about everything I was learning."

She moved the file around. "I let the relationship go further than I should have. I had sex with him. It was a terrible mistake." She lifted her chin and soldiered on. "He became possessive and very jealous. He also began revealing things about his childhood."

Smoke stopped her and asked, "Isn't it odd for a serial killer to have a girlfriend?"

George responded. "No, not really, many do. For example, Douglas Rader, better known as BTK, Yates, Popkova, and Ridgeway aka. the Green River Killer were all married and Ted Bundy had two girlfriends who he professed to love."

She opened the file but didn't read from the page. "One of the assignments for my internship at Quantico was to do a profile on a random subject. I don't know why, maybe something I saw and subconsciously suppressed, but in any case, I choose Hamilton Lighter as my subject. This was the profile I wrote."

She began to read. "Hamilton Lighter, born in Dayton, Ohio to Bryan Lighter and Mary Suffolk Lighter. He was an only child. The father came from a lower-middle-class family. He was smart, handsome and charming but also a grifter who made a living at poker and hustling golf games and tennis matches at country clubs. The father met Mary Suffolk who was the sole heiress to the Suffolk oil fortune, courted, and married but soon fell out of favor when he failed to conform to the Suffolk way of life. The mother became an alcoholic and violent. Hamilton was raised largely by servants who were replaced with regularity. At age six, he was sent to boarding school where there were incidents of bullying, vandalism, and animal cruelty. At ten he returned to the family estate in Dayton where he was home-schooled. Hamilton's IQ tested at 165. He speaks French and Spanish and is something of a mathematics savant."

She turned a page without looking up. "There are no public records on him until he obtained a driver's license at age seventeen. Three days after receiving it, he totaled a new Porsche 911 while under the influence. The year following the accident he was arrested and released five times. No charges were brought and all of the arrest records were sealed. I contacted one of the arresting officers who told me he brought in Lighter twice for stalking and threatening a local girl. Calls were made. Attorneys showed up and he was released without being charged."

She took a breath and continued. "Shortly, after his last arrest, his mother died. She left her entire estate to her son, cutting out her husband completely. Two months after the will was read, the father committed suicide. Hamilton's behavior changed completely. There were no more arrests and he began volunteering at the homeless shelter where he became a valued asset both for his time and his donations."

Smoke looked up at George who was studying him intently.

Olivia continued the history. "Hamilton left Dayton for Cal Tech where he excelled in Statistical Mathematics. After a year at the top of his class, he suddenly transferred to the University of Virginia switching majors from math to philosophy."

She turned the next page. "I was doing a profile, so I needed to dig further into his background. I went to the Dayton police records and looked for unsolved crimes. There were three unsolved murders in the surrounding area. All were girls between sixteen and eighteen, all were raped and killed. The murders took place in different counties and only investigated by local police. No connection was made and the FBI was not involved. I then looked at unsolved murders around Pasadena, California, near Cal Tech. I found three with MO's exactly the same as Dayton."

George coughed interrupting the conversation. "I read Olivia's report. The research was sound as were her conclusions so I assembled a team to verify her findings. In that effort, I had two agents pick up Mr. Lighter and bring him to Quantico for an interview." He lowered his voice and spoke slowly. "That was a huge mistake. He knew Olivia was an intern here and I saw instantly he knew Olivia had betrayed him. The interview had only just begun when attorneys from DC showed up and demanded his immediate release."

Olivia covered Smoke's hand with hers. "George took all the right steps. He put me in protective custody, in a safe house at Quantico, but what neither of us knew was my sister had planned a surprise visit. Lighter must have been waiting for me outside my dorm. Olive, my twin sister, got to campus that evening. She was walking to my apartment when he jumped out and he killed—."

George finished. "There were no eyewitnesses. The local police notified Olivia who called me. A warrant was issued and the police arrested him at his apartment. He had scrubbed with bleach, showered, and the clothes he wore were not immediately found. Later, a canine crew discovered them in a hollow tree behind his apartment."

Smoke took the file and closed the cover. "So, he was tried and convicted but the obvious question is, how did he get out?"

George had the answer. "This man is probably the richest man you'll ever meet. A confidential source inside the firm handling his estate said it is almost physically impossible for him to spend more money per day than his estate makes. So, it follows that his legal team was the best money could buy. He was tried in Virginia on one count of second-degree murder. His lawyers overwhelmed the county District Attorney with motions who, outmanned and outgunned, accepted a temporary insanity plea. The presiding judge, however, was not as pliable as the DA. She allowed the plea but imposed a minimum of seven years under doctor's supervision before a release would be reviewed. He was sent to Central State Hospital for the Criminally Insane."

Olivia picked back up. "That place was built in 1850 and has a horrific history. I'm not sure what happens to serial killers in those institutions, but I'm... certain... that Hamilton Lighter holds me solely responsible for his time behind those walls."

Olivia and George, the rendition of facts complete, waited on Smoke to weigh in.

Smoke took a moment then asked, "Why the show, George, and why did you withhold the last panel of evidence?"

"When a murder occurs, that single investigation becomes the epicenter, the starting point, everything emanates from that case. Local detectives will look first to spouses, known associates... a local cause and effect situation. Only after that is exhausted will some reach out and look for similarities of other cases. Single investigations are often ongoing in multiple locations, without any connection to each other. Years can go by without anyone connecting the dots. However, recently, a new program was introduced to the FBI that, unlike a normal epicenter investigation, provides information in reverse order. The program analyzes all reported crimes from every state. It sorts by category, like missing persons. Hair color, age, profession, sex, weight, political view, religion, anything and everything is sorted and grouped."

Smoke tapped his finger. "Including family history."

"Exactly," George pointed. "A week ago, I read a report that had sixteen missing persons with three things in common: all were female, same age, and all had a twin sister. I immediately put teams on every case, in every state, and confirmed my deduction— they were all committed by Hamilton Lighter."

"The dead body in the last section... the man?"

"Yes, the last section." George folded his hands on the table. "I think Lighter made plans long before his release. The first ones were practice, but he always leaves the same clues. I think he expected it to take a long time to put the pieces together which gave him time to plot and perfect his methods. But now he wants the game to start. He wants us to know it's him."

Olivia spoke up. "Sociopaths have little regard for their own safety. Lighter doesn't believe he can be caught." Her face was pale. "And...he wants me to be afraid."

Smoke directed his attention to George. "The man. Why kill a man and leave the body?"

George answered quickly. "I believe it was part of the message. He is saying he knows you are protecting her. I think the message is, he is going to kill you first then kidnap and kill Olivia."

Both Smoke and Olivia were silent.

"You still haven't told us why you went through with the speech and showing us the evidence room?"

"For my plan to work, I needed to know you were as good as they say you are, Smoke. Olivia will be exposed and the FBI will not be able to protect her." George looked at Olivia. "If you agree to help, Smoke will be your first line of defense."

Smoke turned to Olivia. "He wants you to be the bait."

She looked to George. "If I don't agree?"

"I fear Lighter will intensify his attacks on other women. In fact, he might have already started."

Smoke leaned toward Olivia.

"He's right, O." Smoke's intensity grew. "He's already coming and has the advantage. Hiding isn't much of an option. He'll just wait, maybe a month maybe two, but he will come There isn't much of a choice here but this is an absolute... no other poor unsuspecting girl needs to die because together we are going to put this monster down."

She stared blankly into the distance, then turned and nodded. "I'm in."

6

Diane Copula's trademark red hair was hanging loosely to the side of her head. Her free hand held a microphone that, at the moment, was useless. She was waiting, impatiently, with a hand on her hip and a made-up, camera-ready face reflecting her dissatisfaction with the lackluster performance of her crew. "Are you ready yet?"

The segment producer/director, Dale Maxwell, looking exasperated, responded. "Listen, if he doesn't white balance the camera, you'll look like Ann Coulter in a flour factory."

The cameraman snickered.

Diane Copula paid no attention. She was looking at her reflection in the glass of the Federal Building. Her reputation as a nasty bitch was overshadowed by her ratings as the number one news/beat/gossip/columnist/reporter in New York City.

Her phone buzzed. “What?”

She had given a janitor a hundred dollars and a picture of Doctor Bennet and promised a hundred more if he called and told her what exit door the doctor was going to use.

She pushed disconnect and yelled to Maxwell. “They are coming out the front door. I need that fucking camera, now.”

Maxwell rushed ahead of her and the cameraman. The soundman, carrying a boom-mike, extended a coil of cable as he brought up the rear.

Maxwell pointed to an angle in the building’s exterior that provided cover for an ambush. He positioned the cameraman, then waved Copula to the front of the line. She leaned forward, like a runner, set in position, waiting for the starter’s gun.

The front door was pushed open by a long arm in a well-seasoned corduroy jacket.

“Now.” Maxwell waved a hand like John Wayne leading a cavalry charge.

Coppola sprinted forward, microphone extended and mouth roaring. “Doctor Bennet, Dr. Bennet, why were you called into FBI headquarters?”

Smoke was caught off guard but managed to get an arm in front of the charging reporter.

Copula’s free hand tried to push Smoke’s arm down. She was unsuccessful. “Are you here in connection with an investigation of Hamilton Lighter?”

Doctor Bennet’s head snapped around toward the reporter. She didn’t respond but the TV camera caught the look of shock on her face.

Maxwell stepped into Smoke's path, attempting to block an escape.

With his left arm still blocking the reporter, Smoke extended his right arm straight out. He made an angled fist and pressed his thumb into the knuckle of his first finger. Together, the two appendances became a weapon. With Doctor Bennet at his side, Smoke stuck the point of his fist into the producer/director's solar plexus.

Air from Maxwell's lungs escaped involuntarily and he started to fall backwards. One of his arms, flailing the air and trying to regain his balance, tangled with the soundman's cable. Now lost to gravity, he fell and the cable around his arm ran out of slack, snapped taunt and enveloped Copula' waist.

The reporter didn't notice. "Dr. Bennet, did you—."

When Maxwell hit the ground, the cable pulled on Copula like the cord on a window shade.

The cameraman continued shooting, but not fast-moving Dr. Bennet. He trained the lens on the nasty-bitch reporter who was flying in the air, mouth open and hair flying. She landed hard, arms and legs akimbo, and cursing like a sailor on leave. He kept his finger on the trigger focusing as she bounced, smiling. "What a great day."

This time the click of the limo door was the sound of safety.

Dr. Bennet sighed relief.

"You okay?" Smoke touched her hand.

"Yes, of course." She waved off his concern. "Nice move back there."

"A humorous result from a standard defensive position."

She seemed unconvinced. "Uh, huh."

"Really, it is. It's a Karate hand position called a sword hand. Give me your hand, I'll show you."

He took her hand, shaped her fist, and placed the thumb and finger.

"It's especially effective in close. You can target an eye, the Adams Apple, the scrotum— soft tissue targets."

"I'll keep it in mind."

He moved the conversation from the silly to the important. "So, a TV reporter and crew are waiting for us to emerge from a meeting with the FBI. Obviously, they were tipped. It didn't come from us, so the tip could have only come from one of two places. The FBI, which seems unlikely, or—."

"Lighter." She finished his thought.

"I agree. I think it matches up with what you said sociopaths will do. He wants to be the center of attention."

"But how did he know we would be there today?"

He spun around. "I have to check our phones."

"A bug?"

"It's possible." He turned to face her. "Listen, we have to consider every possibility, hash and rehash every detail. We can't afford to make a mistake."

She didn't seem upset. There was a determined look in her eyes. "So, tomorrow when he sees the headline in the paper, it begins."

The fear Smoke had seen in her before had disappeared. "Yes."

O became pensive. "If I hadn't...I mean, it was just an exercise for my internship. I had a choice of subjects to use in that profile. I could have pulled a random name from the FBI files or even somebody out of the phone book but for some reason, I picked him. He was a boyfriend and I didn't know that much about his background. Even so, I think the reason I chose him was more than just curiosity... it was something else."

"Instinct."

"That may be but it doesn't change the fact I did alert the FBI to Lighter. For that betrayal, he tried to kill me... but he killed my twin sister."

"That's true, that happened, but you have to recognize your report also saved lives."

She snapped around and stared at him. "Really? My sister and sixteen girls are dead. How did I save anybody?"

"You identified him as a serial killer when he was just twenty-four. He'd already killed six times before he met you. Ask yourself, how many would he have killed if he went undetected? Fifty, a hundred, two hundred? The reality is, he was put away for seven years. He's a really rich, really smart guy who could have eluded capture his whole life. The system and his lawyers got him out but without you intervening the way you did he might have never been identified for what he is."

Her eyes welled up. "He killed my sister."

"I know."

Her eyes narrowed. “I want revenge.”

“I can make that happen.”

7

Flannigan's was a small, quiet restaurant with good food and a well-stocked bar. The dinner crowd had not yet arrived and Felix Upton Grant was the lone patron, sitting at the marble topped bar with a cold Molson. He was reading an article in the *New York Post* speculating on whether or not the Jets would finish the year with the same optimism as there was when the season began. One of the very few benefits of the Covid-19 pandemic was the shortened season schedule which spared the team's steadfast fans prolonged pain.

The bartender, putting bottles in a cooler at the end of the bar, pulled his Giant's facemask aside. "You okay?"

"I'm good, Freddie." Felix gave a wave.

"How's David? Haven't seen you guys in here for a while."

"He's been really busy but he's meeting me here in a bit."

The front door opened, and light from the outside lit the front of the restaurant. Three men, un-masked, thirty-somethings, came in, single file. They wore western cut suits with bolo ties and the shortest of the three was sporting a white Stetson cowboy hat. It appeared this wasn't their first stop as their walk was more of a wobble. The group sauntered up to the bar, taking the closest three stools to the door. The one with blond hair yelled out, "Three Johnny Blacks up, draft back. We're celebrating."

The bartender looked at Felix, rolled his eyes, and walked toward the new customers.

Felix studied the arrivals for a few seconds, then went back to his newspaper.

Freddie poured Johnny Walker Black whiskey into a chrome mixer filled with ice, shook it, then poured three perfectly level shots for the new arrivals.

"Shaken not stirred." The blond one clicked his glass with the others as they toasted their...whatever they were celebrating. Breathless from the blast of alcohol, he circled a finger commanding another round from Freddie.

Light from the door illuminated the front again. David Anderson walked in, stopped at the edge of the light, spotted Felix, and walked on.

Felix couldn't help but compare the cowboys with his David. First, he wore a mask which was responsible. They wore suits, as did David, but his man, unlike the unruly, wore the shit out of his.

Felix signaled Freddie, pointed to his bottle, and held up two fingers. The bartender nodded.

David put a hand on Felix's shoulder, leaned down and kissed his cheek before sitting down.

Instantly, at the other end of the bar, one of the men coughed and their conversation, although unintelligible, became slightly louder in volume.

Felix knew what they were talking about. So did David.

Freddie delivered the beer. "Do you want a table; Prime rib is the special."

"Not yet, we're waiting on two more."

Felix slid a coaster around on the bar. "I'm certain Smoke will be glad you could get away early. He called just before you came in and asked me if you were here yet."

"Hmmm. Things must have changed from the, 'Hey let's get together for a drink cause we'll be down your way' invitation."

"I suspect you're right. He sounded pretty serious."

The front door opened, they looked up hopefully, but it was two women carrying shopping bags. The women were thirtyish, attractive and laughing. A waitress approached and directed them to a table. The men at the bar said something in their direction and the two women asked to move. They picked a table away from the drinkers and closer to Felix and David.

Felix picked up where they left off. "O was asked to give a lecture to new recruits at the FBI building."

"Doesn't sound too ominous." David sipped his newly arrived beer.

The three western suits, now five Johnny Walkers later, sauntered from their stools toward the women.

"Afternoon ladies, my friends and I are new in New York. Yep, we're in from Houston, Texas." The blond man seemed to be the spokesman.

One of the two women appeared to be adept. "Welcome to New York, but we're here for dinner and... privacy."

"Ohhhhh." The shorter, dark haired man laughed. "Whoa, shot down, partner."

The blond one, undeterred, tried again. "Ladies, ladies... my friends and I think you two are, what we call in Houston, party girls. So, how about it, you two ready to have some Texas style fun?"

The adept woman was taken aback but sputtered out, "Please, go away."

Freddie started around the bar.

Felix held up his hand to the sixty-year-old, overweight, and really pissed off bartender. "Freddie, may I handle this for you?"

Freddie slowed but didn't stop.

"Please." Felix put on a pouty face.

Freddie stopped, hesitated, then nodded. "Okay. Thank you."

David looked at his mate. "Need help?"

"Are you kidding?"

Felix got off his stool and moved toward the disturbance, arriving directly behind the men. "I believe the ladies asked you boys to go away."

The blond guy spun around; Felix was right in front of him. The blond man leaned back, sizing him up.

Felix was older but bigger possessing a thick neck and

wide shoulders. He looked fit. His standout feature was the bleached white, short, spiked hair that was way different than the, all parted on-the-same- side, haircuts of the cowboys from Houston.

The blond guy peeked over Felix's shoulder to see if any help would come from the bar.

David was sitting on his stool, his back to the action.

Encouraged by his numbers, the blond man challenged Felix. "Listen up buttercup, we weren't doing nothin'—just talking. So, why don't you go back to your boyfriend, and we'll finish our conversation with these two fine looking ladies."

His two partners appeared nervous, but were standing strong.

Felix stared straight ahead. "The ladies asked you to leave. Now, I'm asking you to leave."

The blond guy stepped forward, now shoulder to shoulder with the bigger of his buddies. Together they were two feet away from their adversary.

Felix shortened the distance to one foot. "You need to leave."

"Just so you know what you're getting into here, the three of us are in shape and we are, at least, twenty years younger than you. I fought golden gloves in college and Bill here has a brown belt in Ka-ra-tay." He extended Karate into three syllables. "I think we will stay right here, and continue to talk to these party girls while you... go back to your chocolate bunk-buddy over there and finish your Cosmo."

There was a moment of silence.

Then the blond man pushed too far. "Did you hear me, cock jockey?"

David shook his head.

Felix smiled and two of the men's eyes went to his pearly whites. The moment they did, Felix grabbed their crotches and squeezed.

The two women, who had been silent till now, both gasped but not as loudly as the two men.

Felix squeezed a little tighter. "You have two choices, leave temporarily injured, or leave permanently impotent."

The third man spoke for his mute partners. "We will leave, man, right now. Just, please let them go."

Felix released his grip and they immediately bent over holding themselves. The uninjured man pushed his buddies and together they small-stepped to the door.

"Thank you for your cooperation." Felix waved goodbye then turned to the ladies. "Sorry for the inconvenience ladies."

The one that seemed adept said, "May we buy you a drink for your trouble?"

"No trouble and... yes."

As the three men went out the door, Smoke and Doctor Bennet came in.

Smoke squinted, saw David and Felix and waved.

A waitress approached, "Would you like a table or a booth?"

"Booth for four, please." Smoke gestured at them to follow.

When Felix got close, Smoke pointed to the front door. "Somehow, I think you had something to do with the walking wounded that just left."

Felix replied using a bad English accent. "An ever-so slight disagreement concerning the decorum required toward ladies who wish privacy."

Smoke cocked his head. "I'll bet."

Felix brushed past Smoke and bear-hugged O in spite of social distancing.

David hesitated but she threw her arms around him. "Good to see you, David."

The waitress interrupted. "Can I get you started with something from the bar? This round is on the two ladies, for services rendered."

"A slight disagreement?" Smoke ribbed Felix.

Felix shrugged.

There was a little chatter as the main subject was avoided until the drinks arrived.

Smoke relayed what had happened: how O met Hamilton Lighter, how he killed O's sister, Olive, and what George reported about Lighter's latest victims.

Smoke stopped for a moment. "I didn't know about this when I suggested we meet for a drink. At the time, I just thought we should... I mean—"

"Dude," Felix interrupted. "We're here. What else did he say?"

"They want to use O as bait. They think it's the best way to catch Lighter, maybe the only way."

David was the first to speak. "Jesus."

Felix stuck his oversized arm across the table, took her hand, and quickly said, "I'm in."

David followed Felix's lead. "Me too."

O looked at both of her friends, puzzled. "In for what?"

Felix patted her hand and looked at Smoke. "Your protection detail, my dear. I'll take days, nine to five."

David added, "I can take six to midnight."

O sputtered out, "Wait...wait."

Smoke nodded. "Great, I'll take overnight and do the odd hour patrols. Can you both meet for 8:00 a.m. strategy sessions?"

Both nodded, "Roger that."

O voiced her question, again. "What, the hell, are you talking about?"

Smoke looked but didn't answer her. "We also need someone to stay in the apartment 24/7. Not a lethal force just another set of eyes."

"No problem," Felix slapped the table. "I have the perfect person for the job, Gia. Broadway is still out of commission and since ballet in the street hasn't taken off yet she's very available."

"Okay, that's enough." O was pissed. "What the fuck are you all talking about?"

They shut down and Smoke apologized. "I'm sorry."

She nodded but her eyebrows were furrowed and she still looked pissed.

"You need round-the-clock protection until we come up with a game plan. You heard George tell us the FBI can't protect you when you're being used as bait. Their specialty is after a crime happens not before. The black shiny shoes aren't going to help. It's up to us. Us, here at this table. We will be your protection."

O didn't speak at first but the eyebrows eased and her tone changed from angry to concerned. "Yes, that is true, but... putting David, Felix and now, Gia, in harm's way, again—"

"Stop." Three voices cut her off.

Felix spoke for the group. "Have you forgotten we just did this a few months ago?" Felix puffed his chest. "You know we are badass."

David, smiling a little, shook his head.

O, not smiling, looked at Smoke. "What I remember perfectly is, both of us got shot."

"True, but both of us are still here and those bad guys are not." Smoke then tried humor to relieve her of guilt. "Besides, you know how much these two knights in shining armor love a good battle. In fact, you just saw two of their recent conquests hobble out of here."

O had her head lowered gently shaking it back and forth. She stopped and looked up at the three faces staring at her. "The head of the Behavioral Analysis Unit of the FBI, a man I respect, told us this morning he wants to use me to catch a serial killer. He said if I don't act as a goat on a tether, Lighter will continue to kill."

O stopped, looked at all three, then spoke again. "I think

he's right. There doesn't appear to be another option. I'm the bait."

The three faces hadn't blinked. They were listening to a brave person say brave things.

Smoke took her hand and her attention. "There is some good news here. He could have come after you before with no warning. We wouldn't have been prepared and he would have been successful. But now he is giving us warning. He wants—"

"He wants me to be terrified because I betrayed him."

Smoke nodded.

"The girls he has taken are the message. He is going to kidnap, then kill me."

Her faced was flushed but there was steel in her eyes.

Smoke's jaw clenched as he spoke to David and Felix. "The enemy is formidable with unlimited resources. Everything is in play. For example, I'm certain O's phone was cloned. Lighter knew we were at the FBI building today and he arranged for press coverage."

"Get the fuck..." Felix didn't finish his statement of surprise.

"From now on, leave your phones at home. I will give you a new burner phone every morning. We will meet at the SoHo apartment at 0800 every morning. Felix, can you borrow the bug sweeping equipment from your buddy?"

"Roger that."

"Good. I'll get the files from the FBI but it will take time to get a battle plan together. For now, our only assignment is protection."

"Roger that."

Smoke upped the ante. "She is allowed to be afraid. We are not. We have experienced war and our enemy now is the same as it was in battle, fear. I am not talking about courage, that is unquestioned. It is the fear you'll make a mistake, miss a sign, a signal, a face in the crowd. That fear will defeat our planning, and cause a moment of hesitation which he is counting on. We need to expect skirmishes. He will probe our defense, assessing strength, timing, and capability. He will look for weakness."

Smoke looked at O. "Tell them what you told me in the car about a profiler searching for a serial killer."

Her voice cracked a little. "A profiler can work for years to get inside the head of a serial killer who always seems to be just out of reach. That continues until the detective starts thinking like the killer, understanding the MO. When that happens, there is a role reversal and the hunter becomes the hunted."

"Every missing girl on the FBI's radar was taken on the twenty-third of the month." Smoke put both hands flat on the table. "Today is the eleventh. That means Lighter will try to take O fourteen days from today."

8

Fourteen days left
10:30 Pm

The room was dark except for one ceiling fixture casting a conical beam of light on one large picture. It was a blowup of a single frame of film cropped from a twelve-minute, thirty-one- second video. Hamilton Lighter sat in a large soft-leather chair, in the middle of the otherwise empty room, mesmerized.

In negotiations, he agreed to occasional contact with the TV reporter in exchange for information and, most importantly, every frame of film her team captured as a result of his tips. He also made it clear to the reporter any leak to the police of their arrangement would sever their relationship and possibly Diane Copula's red head.

Within three hours of the media ambush outside the FBI building, Diane Copula emailed the raw videotape to his encrypted email address. He played the video on his computer. The questions flew and she seemed unaffected. She had her chin up, and had a confident, self-assured gait right up to when the reporter said, "Are you here in connection with an investigation of Hamilton Lighter?"

He used its software to advance the film slowly, until he found the frame with the exact moment when Olivia Bennet heard the reporter say his name. It captured her clenched jaw, drained white face, and wide eyes, filled with shock and fear. He used the editing function to divide the photo into ten pieces. He then printed each piece of the frame on eight and a half by eleven paper, making one large thirty-two by forty-eight-inch poster. He then hung his work-of- art on the blank wall. The magnified face of Dr. Olivia Bennet was mesmerizing.

The screen on his phone lit up, its caller ID announced Angela Bower, his executive assistant. Lighter never met his assistant. Every conversation, every task, every transaction was done by phone or encrypted email. There was no office, no paper, no IP address, and no traceable connection to him. All deliveries were to blind addresses and all monetary transactions were through off-shore, numbered accounts. She didn't know what he looked like, his history, or even his name.

Lighter knew everything about her.

Bower was a middle-aged, single woman with no family. She had an impressive resume, except for a single flaw. She was agoraphobic. Her fear of going outside her home was a result of post traumatic syndrome suffered after a brutal mugging and rape. The affliction was paralyzing and absolute. Her single flaw made her practically unemployable to everyone but Lighter. To him, Angela Bower was a perfect employee.

The phone vibrated again. He pushed the green Accept icon. "Is everything arranged?"

"Yes, sir. Six prepaid phones will be delivered to the concierge at your address in twenty minutes." She stopped speaking— she knew to wait.

He took a cigar from a humidor on the table next to his chair, removed his lighter, and flipped the lid. Something that was supposed to happen, didn't. He stared at the unlit filament. His $79,000 lighter didn't work on the first try. His cheeks flushed with anger.

"Call whomever you bought this piece of shit lighter from and have them send someone to fix it. It didn't light. I'll leave it with the concierge."

There was silence on the line.

"Do you understand?" He said it slowly, emphasizing each word.

She stammered, "Yes sir. Right away, sir. I will contact Cartier, immediately."

He closed then flipped the lid again. The flame appeared.

Piece of shit.

Lighter sucked air through the tobacco until the end of

the cigar was glowing red. The lid snapped when it closed, and he tossed the lighter to the table. He exhaled and looked through the grey smoke at Olivia's face, refocusing his rage.

He spoke calmly. "I need this apartment for two, possibly three more days."

"I understand." Her voice a little shaky but regaining confidence.

"Did you arrange for the clean?"

"Yes. The usual crew will remove and destroy the furniture—clothes, the chair, the bed and anything else left behind, then bleach and scrub every surface."

"You have confidence?"

"I do. They know there will be an inspection and understand there would be consequences for betrayal."

The word caused his eye to flinch.

He drew on the cigar again. "I'll need cash."

"Amount?"

"Twenty thousand, usual denominations."

"Tomorrow morning, immediately after the bank opens, delivered by secure messenger to the concierge, under the name Harold Shipman."

He had given her a new name to use each time a delivery was made. This time he chose the man known as Doctor Death, an English physician who killed 250 patients before being discovered.

"Do you have a new encrypted email account?"

"Yes. I'll text the address to the new prepaid phone when you log on. They all have the usual access code."

More silence.

He toyed with playing with her, but thought better of it. It was too close to the end. A game now might be a distraction for a person of lesser intelligence and would disrupt the pattern. He had to have pattern...consistency...predictability.

She broke silence first. "How was the flight?"

Her comment caught him by surprise. His jet landed at Opa-Locka airport near Miami and he took a private charter to Republic Airport in Farmingdale outside of NYC. His passport date stamped him back into the US. It documented his arrival from Milan in Miami, not New York. The private charter didn't require a name.

"The car was five minutes late."

"I apologize, sir." She waited for a response then, in its absence, filled the gap. "I will be available for you at any time, sir."

"Yes, you will." He pushed the red disconnect icon.

Lighter laid his head back, and fired the glow on the cigar. He closed his eyes then parted his lips, letting a pewter mist slowly escape. He believed everyone could be bought, that there was an amount, that buys even the most righteous person's compliance. He also came to recognize that it is better to understand the payment to be rent rather than ownership. Once wealth beyond expectations is achieved, the fear of losing it becomes more powerful than the offer of more money.

The pilots and the crew accepted their fortune, taking every abuse, and every dollar. They knew his face, knew dates, time and destinations and now that his plan was coming to conclusion, they were all loose ends.

He put the faulty lighter in his pocket, checked his watch, and left Olivia's picture for the bedroom. A single lamp on a small nightstand was next to a king-size bed covered with pure white sheets. A red comforter folded diagonally lay at its foot. The sheets were Merlino, which he favored over the cloth of Porthault Jours de Paris. The latter used the best cotton in the world, but he found Merlino's wool fabric, woven with small amounts of gold carat and a silk jacquard, to be more to his liking, mostly because they were $2,400 dollars a set, as opposed to $2,000. He would use them twice.

He rolled the cigar in his fingers and the ash fell unnoticed, as he walked to the floor-to-ceiling windows which afforded a museum quality view of the New York City skyline.

The night was clear and, since the pandemic generated exodus, only a small portion of the windows were lit. Now, because of the city's diminished illumination, only shadowed outlines of buildings rose into the night sky. Stars that heretofore were never seen descended to the roof tops and peeked out from the gaps between the structures.

He pressed his hand to the glass—fingers stretched out, knuckles white. Her building's silhouette was right there, three blocks away. He could see her window.

She knows I'm coming.

She changed his life and now, finally, he would change hers.

Nothing could stop him, not the police, not the FBI, and certainly not her bullshit protection. Nothing could stop him from exacting the price of her betrayal.

He thought of a second picture of her face and his knuckles relaxed. It would be of the exact moment of her death.

9

Thirteen days left

5:00 Am

Smoke turned the handle on the bedroom door as quietly as possible. He winced when it clicked. O was asleep, and he wanted her to stay that way. He left slowly, pausing in the doorway, ogling her. He couldn't help himself. It was a little more than a year since they first met and he still found himself staring.

I'm the luckiest bastard in the world.

One slightly bent leg poked out from under the sheet. It was long, shapely and partially covered with a cobalt blue silk nightgown. Her head rested on white sheets she had pulled tight to her chin. He knew what was underneath the sheet, which was why he couldn't stop staring. He slowly closed the door behind him then sat to put on the boots he had carried out of the bedroom. A black hoodie completed his ensemble.

A man in a dark suit and a white curly antenna wire in his ear stood to the right of the door when he exited the apartment.

"Morning, Agent...?"

"Dobler, Special Agent Dobler, sir."

"Sorry, Special Agent. What's the deployment?"

"I have this floor; Agent Franks is on the roof, and Agent Happ is in the lobby."

"You're in charge, Special Agent Dobler?"

"Correct."

Smoke sized him up. "Okay, I'll do the perimeter, now. Is it necessary to alert Agent Happ I'm coming down?"

"No, sir. We've been briefed."

Smoke stepped to him. "Keep alert." He paused then added sincerely, "Please."

The agent gave him a confident nod. "We got this."

The elevator opened and he immediately spotted the FBI agent whose attempt at an undercover disguise was wearing a concierge's jacket. However, his shiny black shoes were visible from the space station.

Smoke passed by. "Agent."

Happ sputtered with surprise, "Ah...ah."

Smoke stopped for a moment when he reached the front

door. He looked through the glass both ways, pushed it opened, and stepped quickly onto the nearly empty sidewalk. Starting his perimeter check by circling the block, he turned right.

Across the street, on the steps down to the subway, he spotted a barely visible bald head, eye-high to the sidewalk. It was a big head with an unusual shape. It resembled the top half of an unspent bullet.

Smoke walked to the end of the block, crossed the street, and turned right.

Bullethead came up the stairs and followed but didn't cross to get behind Smoke. Instead, he stayed on the opposite side of the street.

Slowing his pace, Smoke used reflections in window glass and quick glances to observe his tail. There was a big body attached to the bald head. It was four inches taller and fifty pounds heavier so Smoke began looking for an advantage— a vulnerability.

Smoke came to the end of the block and started crossing to the other side of the street.

It was a move that caught Bullethead off-guard. The tail stopped quickly, pretending to window shop.

Amateur.

Smoke was able to get a good look. If this guy got a first shot, it would be big trouble, best not to let that happen.

Halfway into the crosswalk, the man started walking toward him and Smoke spotted the advantage he was looking for. The man was extremely bowlegged. He wore boots with badly slanted, worn down soles that made him lean to one side when he took a step. It wasn't much, but given the man's size it might be Smoke's only advantage.

Smoke picked up the pace to something just short of a trot. He turned the next corner and ducked into an alley. He heard the boots coming.

Bullethead passed the opening and Smoke stepped out, put his right hand on the bigger man's back, and pushed hard.

The man stumbled but didn't fall.

Smoke stepped back into the alley.

Bullethead followed.

No words were spoken but the intent was clear.

They squared off.

Smoke took a right-handed boxer's position—balls of his feet, hands up, left foot slightly forward.

Bullethead's arms were at his side with both hands rolled into fists. His eyes were fixed on his target, Smoke.

Smoke stood still, coiled like a cat ready to strike a mouse.

Bullethead moved first. He stepped with his left foot, his right fist following behind.

It was Smoke's moment of advantage.

Bullethead's weight landed full on the slanted heel. Everything he had was leaning right.

Smoke countered, moving left. His head and shoulders lowered slightly.

Bullethead's fist flew by Smoke's chin, missing by a centimeter.

Smoke's center of gravity was low. With his legs and hips driving his weight up, his left fist accelerated into a short powerful uppercut that made flush contact with Bullethead's eighth, ninth, and tenth ribs. Smoke heard nine and ten break, and from the way Bullethead crumbled, he assumed one of them might have stuck in the lung.

Bullethead backed up against the alley wall and slid to the ground, holding his side. His mouth was open— no sound came out.

Smoke stood for a moment, still at the ready, but the man was incapacitated.

He dropped his fists and leaned in a bit. "Who hired you?"

Bullethead didn't speak.

"You didn't say anything before you attacked. There was no, 'give me your wallet'. No, 'you fucked my sister'. Nothing. You don't know me. So... tell me, who hired you?"

Bullethead's mouth was still open and soundless.

Smoke moved a toe toward the busted ribs.

There was a weak protest. "Nooo, wait."

Smoke pulled back.

Bullethead pointed to his jacket pocket.

Smoke cautiously patted it, reached inside, then withdrew a photo. It was black and white and had been taken that morning when he and O were walking out of the FBI building.

"Who hired you?"

Bullethead shook his head.

"Who?" Smoke tapped the broken ribs with his toe.

"AHHHHHHHHH."

"Who?"

Bullethead shook his head again.

"Was it Hamilton Lighter?"

There was no recognition in the man's eyes, only pain.

Smoke believed him. He didn't know who hired him.

Bullethead opened his mouth, a weak voice eked out, "Hospital."

Smoke considered the request. He put the picture in his pocket. "Listen, I'm not unsympathetic toward your condition, however, there's the whole you trying to kill me, thing."

The man's face was silently pleading.

"Okay...I'll call 911. It might take a while for them to get here and I do feel bad leaving you here in such pain." Smoke smiled kinda sideways. "How about a little anesthetic?"

Smoke half-kicked the ribs and Bullethead passed out.

10

Thirteen days left

8:15 Am

Everyone had a cup of coffee. The strategy meeting hadn't begun. One participant was overdue.

Felix leaned forward in a chair undersized for his frame and tapped his cup, impatiently. He looked at Smoke. "You sure he's coming?"

David, checking his watch, also seemed antsy.

Gia and O were catching up, and didn't seem interested in the time.

A loud knock got Smoke up and to the door. The peephole revealed George DiSanto and his dusty cardigan sweater.

George nodded, walked past Smoke, and addressed O who had come out of the kitchen to greet her old boss. "I apologize for my tardiness. I was detained on an unexpected but related incident." George shot a glance at Smoke who responded with a shrug.

Smoke stepped toward the group and pointed to the late arrival. "Everyone, this is George DiSanto. He heads the Behavioral Analysis Unit of the FBI. George, this is our team: Felix Upton Grant, David Anderson, and Gia. We have worked together in the past—"

"I'm aware of your past and I've been briefed on your associates."

Felix and David were surprised.

Smoke was not.

Gia smiled. "George, would you like some coffee?"

He gave her a polite nod then addressed the group. "There was an incident early this morning that caused me to be late. It happened just around the corner from here. I was notified by the NYPD because we have an operation in their jurisdiction."

George turned to Smoke. "Do you want to fill me in on the man who assaulted you this morning? I got the NYPD version. I'd like to hear yours."

All heads turned toward Smoke, surprised.

"At approximately 5:15 a.m., I initiated a two-block perimeter check. I was looking for anything out of the ordinary, like cars or vans parked for surveillance or suspicious street vendors. When I came out of the door, I saw a man... actually, I saw just the top of a man's head, across the street, hiding on the stairs leading down to the subway. I started down the block and he followed me. I turned a corner and ducked into an ally. He followed and tried to take me down but I disabled him."

George choked on a sip of coffee. "You broke two ribs and dislocated another, apparently with a single blow. He's at Belleview getting his lung re-inflated."

Smoke continued unabashed. "Yeah, I got lucky, but more importantly, he had this on him." Smoke pulled out the picture he took from the man and handed it to George.

George examined it carefully. "Not photograph paper... standard printer... fresh. It's likely it was printed from an emailed file." George walked to the door, opened it, and leaned into the hallway. He handed the photo to Agent Dobler, gave him instructions and returned to the group.

George continued. "Smoke, have you seen that man before?"

"No, I would have remembered him. He had a very distinguishing feature—a big, odd-shaped, bald head."

George removed his phone, scrolled, then spun the screen around for O and Smoke. "Does the name Delmont Tuti sound familiar to either of you?"

Both shook their heads.

"The NYPD identified the man and sent me his rap sheet. Mr. Tuti was arrested three times, with one conviction, all assaults. He was employed by a company that has a contract to supply security personnel to government facilities in Virginia."

"He was fired for abusing patients when he was a guard at..." George paused letting the anticipation build. "Central

State Hospital for the Criminally Insane in Petersburg, Virginia"

O breathed out, "He knows Lighter."

George nodded. "Tuti was employed at the hospital during the last two years of Lighter's internment. My agents will work to establish a connection, like if he worked on Lighter's floor, supervised a work detail, etcetera. But it is possible Lighter only knew of his violent reputation and never actually met him. He could have contacted Tuti after he was fired."

Smoke addressed Felix and David on a different point. "I told you about the crime boards of evidence that George put up at our meeting at the FBI office."

Felix and David nodded.

"There were fifteen missing person reports posted. Number sixteen was withheld." Smoke turned to George. "Number sixteen... the reports on the white board you didn't post... it was like the others... a missing person, a woman with a twin sister. There was a girl taken, a twin, like the others but this time there was a body associated with the kidnapping— a man."

George nodded. "Keep going."

"When O and I arrived for the meeting, you identified the agents in attendance. They were all from different cities and all of them were associated with one of the murders, except one. The unidentified agent was from Miami... number sixteen, correct?"

"Yes, number fifteen happened in Miami."

"The man from this morning, the former guard, Tuti, he lived in Miami before working at the hospital?"

"Yes."

Felix and David were observing the exchange like one watching a tennis match.

Smoke rose and began pacing.

George drank more coffee.

Smoke asked George another question. "The man was not the missing girl's boyfriend?"

"She was a dancer at a strip club and he was the bouncer."

"A bodyguard, then?"

George nodded.

"How was the boyfriend/bodyguard killed?"

"Beaten to death."

Smoke sat down next to O. "So, it is likely Lighter hired Tuti to kill the bodyguard so he would have the opportunity to kidnap the girl without interference." He looked at O. "It was a trial run to perfect details for when Tuti kills me before Lighter tries to abduct you."

George agreed. "Possible."

"Tuti was following me but I spotted him, probably screwing up Lighter's plan."

George mulled on that for a bit.

The others were waiting for the next chapter to begin.

"Lighter stared today. The deal with that reporter is the start of his attempt to get to you and put a tail on me to test the water here in New York."

George put a hand on Olivia's shoulder. "I agree with

Smoke, Olivia. I think he wants the press involved because he wants to instill fear in you."

O looked up with fire in her eyes. "You two remember what I do for a living, right? This man wants to seem invincible. He's a narcissist who lives for these moments."

Felix stood up. "So, that's enough, right... all the evidence you have and now he turns this bullethead guy loose and I mean can't the FBI just pick this guy up and stick him back where he belongs?"

George shook his head. "No. There is no evidence to charge him with anything. It is most probable there will not be any evidence linking Lighter to Tuti."

Everyone was quiet.

Gia suddenly bounced in from the kitchen. "Breakfast is ready. I made huevos rancheros and cornbread muffins." Her smile met sullen faces, and she dejectedly returned to her duties.

David spoke. "What's next, Smoke? What can we do? I mean, you were attacked by this former guard this morning. Doesn't that mean Lighter is in New York and ready to try to take O?"

Smoke pointed to David, opened his mouth to speak, then stopped and turned back to George. He stood still a moment, silent, then pointed. "George, do you have all the files on the first missing person case?"

George looked puzzled. "I do. I brought the agents-in-charge to the meeting. They gave me a full briefing and a copy of everything they have. If you need the files, I can have them delivered."

Smoke mumbled, "Yes, please." He started pacing again.

The group was quiet and looked at each other wondering what Smoke would say next. Even FBI section chief George DiSanto, who technically was in charge, joined the group's puzzled state.

Gia returned to the room holding a wooden spoon in the air. "Listen up, if you fuckers don't come in here and eat right now, I'm going to have to throw it all in the garbage. You can't eat cold eggs. It's against the law." Even when she tried to act angry, Gia looked happy.

Smoke, his trance broken, smiled a little. "Yes, we should eat. David, do you have any vacation time coming?"

"Yes, two weeks, actually."

"Great. Can you be ready to leave tomorrow?"

David, along with everyone else, went from puzzled to baffled. "I guess so. Where are we going?"

"Hawaii."

11

Thirteen days left

11:15 Am

George DiSanto was uncomfortable in this office. Unlike Quantico, the New York City's bureau office was a metropolitan high-rise and too orderly. He preferred low country rural and messy. Making things worse, he was standing over the shoulder of the only man in the employ of the FBI who was actually older than he was. The man was staring at a series of three computer screens lined up next to each other, all of them had lines of code streaming from top to bottom.

The seated man spoke. "You have no idea what you're looking at, so why are you standing here annoying me?"

"I know what you're doing. I just don't know how you're doing it."

"Same thing. You're bugging me. Go away."

The man with his fingers dashing across the keyboard was Harry Serpico, a legend amongst those in the computer science world. He was retired by the FBI when he reached the mandated retirement age of fifty-seven but since then he hadn't missed a day's work. For ten years, Serpico worked as a private contractor and continued to be the BAU's secret weapon. Serpico didn't fit the mold, not unlike George. George didn't wear suits and ties and Serpico wasn't a pimply kid with unwashed hair, thick glasses, and a fetish for all things Star Wars. But both men possessed important foundational talent.

George patted Harry's shoulder. "Can you break it?"

Harry turned and gave George the same look he always did when he asked the same stupid question.

George patted the shoulder again and headed to his office.

The code he was working on was from a private email service that had refused to give access, preventing his agents from determining where a particular subscriber was located. The Patriot Act allows for moderating most everything broadcast for certain key words in fifty different languages to head off a terrorist attack.

In pursuit of Mr. Hamilton Lighter, George got a few additional words added to the search parameters and some success was realized. He applied for a warrant for the encrypted email service, but the judge denied it stating, although a threat, Lighter did not fit the legal definition of a terrorist and cautioned George against violating the constitutional rights of a citizen.

The judge's decision made George angry, an emotion he almost never allowed. He was fifty-seven, three months short of his own mandatory retirement but looked sixty-seven. He made his career playing by the rules however he was tired of following every rule and regulation. He liked Olivia, blamed himself for what happened to her sister and he was angry. So, George made a decision. Lighter was a monster who used money and power to escape justice. Hamilton Lighter was not a citizen worthy of constitutional protection, he was a terrorist and a mass murderer.

George overruled the judge and called on Harry Serpico to work some off-the-books magic. He needed Harry to find a single light in the colorless depths of the internet. He needed answers. He needed to stop his friend from being kidnapped and murdered.

He picked up the phone and hit a new contact number.

Smoke answered on the first buzz. "George."

"When are you leaving?"

"We have tickets on United tomorrow at 8:30 arriving in Honolulu at 2:30 in the afternoon, about a ten-hour flight, non-stop."

"I'll have the local office meet you at the plane."

Smoke's voice rose, commanding. "No, don't do that."

"Why not?"

"I have a plan and it doesn't involve the FBI. George, I respect your work. I admire your agents, but you guys are as easy to spot as thoroughbreds at a pony ride. I got this George."

There was silence on the phone while George had to finally decide to let Smoke be the lead horse. "Okay, where are you staying?"

"The Ali'i at the Hilton Hawaiian Village."

"You realize that is the most public hotel complex in the whole of Hawaii? There are stores, the beach is famous, and the restaurants are public."

"Yes, it's perfect. The Ali'i is expensive, and secure. It would be very hard to kidnap O without being seen. In fact, Diane Copula, that TV reporter that broke the story, is about to get an exclusive."

George was dumbfounded.

"I can hear from your silence, George, you have reservations."

"I do... why?"

"I promise, I have a plan."

George submitted. "What can I do?"

"First be ready. When I call, there won't be much time to respond."

"I'll leave New York as soon as I can set up a command at the local office. Use this number."

"Have you made any progress on finding Lighter?"

"Yes and no. I'm running down some leads which look promising."

"Thanks, George. I know O appreciates you."

"Take care of her."

Harry Serpico burst through the office door with a smile on his face.

George's voice changed to urgent while pushing disconnect. "Gotta go."

Harry continued to smile and now waved a piece of paper.

"What?"

"I got something."

George caught the excitement. "You got into the emails."

"No, not exactly." Harry continued to wave the paper and smile.

"If you don't tell me now, I swear to God I'll shoot you and take the paper from your dead fingers."

"You have no sense of humor." Harry took the paper, adjusted his glasses, and began reading...to himself.

George reached into the desk drawer and removed a thirty-eight pistol.

Harry looked up but wasn't amused.

George cocked the weapon.

Harry gulped then spoke up. "Have you ever heard of a Dupont Ligne Champagne cigar lighter?"

12

Twelve days left
2:30 PM - Pacific time

Black SUV turned off Ala Moana Boulevard into the entrance of the Hilton Hawaiian Village. The ride from Inouye International Airport was quick, much quicker than the pre-Covid bumper- to-bumper traffic into downtown Honolulu.

The vehicle passed a huge bronze gong suspended outside a Benihana two-story restaurant. It went under a gracefully arched wooden pedestrian bridge lined with multi colored flags that led to high-end stores with an abundance of vacation treasures and keepsakes. The architecture was beautiful and the landscaping perfect. Everything was pristine in paradise.

"Aloha." A bellman in a uniform of white shorts and a flowered blue silk shirt opened the rear door of the car.

Smoke's dungaree-covered leg poked out first which caused the perfectly dressed hotel employee to retreat a step. Not only was he dressed for an after-hours bar, he looked like he was on the tail end of a three-day bender. He stretched, rubbed red eyes, and brushed back his uncombed hair with both hands.

When O emerged, the bellman smiled brightly and regained his lost step. "Aloha and welcome to the Hilton Hawaiian Village."

O, unlike Smoke, looked fresh and rested. She'd slept on the plane. Smoke had not.

Gia popped her head out, her eyes wide. "Wow and wow, again."

The driver's door was opened by a second bellman dressed in white and blue. Felix unfolded himself from behind the seat, ducking his white spiked hair out of the door. He was a sight to behold. Hairy legs that were almost as white as his bleached hair stuck out below red and white gym shorts. His color coordinated muscle shirt went unnoticed, overshadowed by the tattoos on arms, shoulders, and back.

Felix put both hands on his hips. "Awesome."

David came around from the passenger side looking like he didn't belong to the group. He was pressed and folded and ready for work, a play or the prom— not a hair out of place, nary an uncreased seam or a wrinkle where it shouldn't be.

The rear lift door opened and bags were withdrawn to waiting bell carts.

"Ali'i Tower." Smoke nodded to the bellman and the people parade followed the cart.

Smoke took a step back, closing in on Felix and David. "Take my flank. We should make contact any time."

Smoke moved to the point position, putting O and Gia behind him, protected by Felix and David, right and left.

The cart went by the penguin pond and passed carts selling sarongs and kika flower leis.

Behind an elephant ear palm tree, Diane Copula waited, microphone at the ready.

Smoke turned to O. "Ready?"

She nodded.

The New York TV reporter burst forward, cameraman following step for step. "Dr. Bennet... Dr. Bennet... are you here in Hawaii to get away from Hamilton Lighter?"

Smoke feigned resistance, sticking out arms blocking the reporter's incoming charge but not the camera angle.

O lifted her chin and calmly replied. "No. I'm...we... are here on vacation."

The redheaded reporter pressed. "There are reports of missing women all matching your description. Hamilton Lighter is rumored to be a suspect in that investigation. Two days ago, you were called into FBI headquarters in New York and then you suddenly left for Honolulu. Doctor Bennet, what is your connection to the Lighter investigation?" Copula was almost breathless when she finished.

The microphone in the reporter's hand got close to O. Too close. Smoke grabbed Copula's wrist and pushed it back.

"There is no connection." O started walking again.

Undaunted, Copula stuck the microphone out again. "Is it true, you ran away from New York because you're afraid of Hamilton Lighter?"

Now, Smoke stopped walking and stepped toward the reporter.

The reporter gave a hand signal to the cameraman who dialed in for a close-up of Smoke's face.

Smoke looked straight at the lens. "Hamilton Lighter is a punk."

Six white and blue garbed hotel workers swarmed the scene and pushed the reporter and her crew back up the path toward the exit.

Smoke took O's hand and they walked toward the entrance of the Ail'i, the very exclusive, well protected Hilton hotel tower. He took a movie star pose, chin up and one furrowed eyebrow. "How was my close-up Mr. DeMille?"

"I don't know if it's an Oscar but pretty sure it's an Emmy winner."

She took his arm and laid her head against his shoulder as they walked.

A ceramic ashtray flew across the room and shattered the TV screen. Pieces of glass fell to the carpet and the light from the TV flickered from bright white to grey then went black.

"Fucking son-of-a-bitch. Mother fucking son-of-a-bitch." Lighter was blind with rage.

I'm a punk! That god damn motherfucker. Punk. Fuck him. Punk." He was spitting. His mind on fire.

The bodyguard turned the reporter he used to ambush Bennet at the FBI office against him.

He stormed around his rented New York apartment's empty room, plotting, thinking, raging.

Next, what's next?

He picked up his phone and dialed his assistant.

Angela Bower answered on the first ring.

"I want a place on Oahu, immediately. You know where. I want a remote, secure location, like before."

"Yes sir."

"Have $50,000 delivered tomorrow morning."

"Yes sir."

There was a pause. He was thinking and she wasn't interrupting.

"I want a complete workup on Diane Copula, channel 7 Action News, New York. Everything, dogs, mother, boss, everything."

"Right away, sir."

"Now, where's my lighter?"

She hesitated for a second, then with pride of accomplishment replied. "The repairman from Tiffany's hung up with me just before you called. The device is repaired and is with the concierge."

Lighter disconnected.

He pressed autodial number two.

"Yes sir." The pilot answered.

"When can you get to Teterboro?"

A moment passed while the pilot calculated the flight time from Miami. "I'll have the plane ready by tomorrow morning."

Lighter checked his watch. "I want wheels up by 9:00 a.m."

"Can do, sir."

"We will have another drop."

"Yes sir. No problem. If we're headed to Europe again, I'll have to notify—"

"No need for that. My destination is Honolulu, Hawaii."

13

Ten days left
5:30 PM - Pacific time

Smoke needed quiet and was pacing in the hallway of the fifteenth floor of Hilton's Ali'i tower. It was narrow and long with one window at its far end. He had his head down, calculating, planning, working on the best defense— an offense. There were twelve doors to rooms on the floor. He assumed they were empty, because only a moron would be inside a hotel room when the sun was still up in Hawaii, unless one was hiding from a relentless serial killer.

The room sheltering Smoke, O, and Gia in luxury was the last door in the row, farthest from the elevator and nearest to the ocean. It was a luxurious two-room suite, with a deck that provided a 180-degree view of the ocean. West, from its balcony, one could see Magic Island and its lagoon providing access to the ocean. Yachts of all descriptions and well used fishing boats and graceful schooners filled the docks. East the view was the wide white sand beaches, buildings forming the skyline of Waikiki and, in the distance, perhaps the most recognizable mountain profile in the world, Diamond Head.

He came to the end of the hall, turning his back to the window which offered a view of a cloudless blue sky. Smoke didn't look out. He was focused. This was a high stakes poker game and O was all the chips in the pot. His plan had to work. There was no room for error. All possibilities needed to be anticipated, considered, and evaluated. But he was doubting himself, doubting the plan because he knew his ability to devise a successful scheme was limited because—he was sane.

Felix poked his head out the door of the room adjacent to O's suite. "Hey, got a minute?"

Smoke nodded.

Felix came out wearing what resembled a swimsuit and a bright red shirt with multi-colored parrots. "David is doing recon. He'll be back in thirty minutes. Do I have time to test the water?"

Smoke shook his head. "Change clothes. I'll need you ready to go when he returns."

"You don't like my ensemble?" Felix grinned and did a model posing hand gesture.

Smoke ignored Felix's attempt at humor. "You and I need to take a ride and I need you to look serious."

Felix looked like he was going to try another joke but didn't. "Sure, no problem. Where we headed?"

"To see an old friend."

Smoke turned away when his phone rang. He pushed the accept icon and Felix ducked back into his room.

"Smoke, I have some good news." George's voice rang clear over the 5,000-mile distance between New York and Honolulu.

"I could use some, but first: did we show up on TV?"

"It's the lead story. Even the other networks ran it."

"Good." Smoke breathed relief.

"So, step one is done and we can assume Lighter knows exactly where Olivia is."

"Yes, I have no doubt he knows we're in Hawaii." Smoke hesitated a moment. "George, I've spent hours looking for the flaw in this plan and I still have reservations. I feel like I'm missing something because I can't anticipate his next move."

"Listen Smoke, the film of you arriving at the hotel in Hawaii has changed our position from defense to offense. It's smart. And... Smoke, now we don't have to think like him. We don't have to anticipate his next move. He has to anticipate ours."

"I know but—"

"Remember when Olivia told the agents in her speech about hesitation causing a second of delay that could be catastrophic? Well, my friend, you need to follow her advice."

Smoke let the wise words sink in.

George changed the subject. "Besides, I told you I had good news."

"Right. What is it?"

George cleared his throat signaling a soliloquy. "I have a

very good team, each talented in very specific ways. One of them is dedicated to breaking down encrypted emails." He lowered his voice a little like he was conveying a secret. "Harry Serpico is not currently FBI. He's former FBI, forced into mandatory retirement just like what's soon to happen to me—"

"George, can you cut to the chase? What's the good news?"

"Right, sorry. Harry wrote an algorithm using a keyword search like what's used in pursuit of terrorists. Normally words like bomb, plastic explosive, and detonator are some of the flash words that can isolate a particular email amongst billions. In this case, we modified the search using keywords specific to this investigation. He looked for words like Bennet, murder, kidnap, abduction, Lighter, or Hamilton. He even used Smoke. What he found was the proverbial needle in a haystack, a one in a million, freak hit. There was a transmission from New York about a lighter... not Lighter with a capitol L... a small l, an actual lighter. Now, an email about a cigarette lighter wouldn't be anything to raise interest. However, the message was transmitted from a highly encrypted email account."

"And?"

"And... a repairman from Tiffany's was to be sent to an apartment building about three blocks from Olivia's condo to fix a cigar lighter." George paused, apparently waiting for a reaction that didn't come. He grunted in disappointment and finished his big reveal. "The lighter cost $75,000 which was paid by wire transfer from a numbered Cayman account.

Tiffany's received the email and a repairman was scheduled, but the customer was anonymous. The repairman was to fix a lighter which was left at the front desk."

"Interesting." Smoke's voice was calm.

"Interesting," George exploded. "Are you kidding? It's Hamilton Lighter. It has to be. Three blocks away from O's condo... a ridiculously expensive lighter and a heavily encrypted, IP address. It has to be Lighter's lighter."

Smoke didn't respond but his mood was altered slightly because he was enjoying playing with O's friend.

A half a minute went by. "George."

"What?"

"You know, I'm just fucking with you."

"Very funny."

"Really George, this is amazing. What are you going to do with the information?"

Smoke heard a long calming breath over the phone.

"First, of course I put a team out for visual confirmation but we also, and this is the best part, we intercepted the repairman before he was dispatched to the building. Our agent will accompany him and will place a small GPS tracking device inside the case. The lighter is battery operated so it will locate him wherever he goes."

"What if Lighter sweeps it?"

"The device sends a single tone every sixty seconds. It draws very little power so there will be no battery issues and the possibility of a sweep device picking up a signal is very remote."

"Excellent."

George asked a question. “How did you manage the TV ambush with the same reporter from New York in Hawaii?”

“O made a call to the station manager, called in a favor, and arranged for the reporter to be sent to the hotel. They used the local affiliate station for cameras and sound equipment. It wasn’t as big a deal as I thought it would be. They were happy about the exclusives.”

“Step one complete.”

Smoke spoke quickly. “Lighter told us he planned to kidnap and kill O on the 25th. We’ve tethered O as bait, but when he tries to come for her, we’ll be ready.”

“Does Olivia agree he’ll still try, even though we have tilted the playing field towards our side?”

“She does. She said he’s a sociopath who doesn’t fear getting caught. He loves attention and in spite of him not being in complete control he will try. Using the same reporter was important because it will piss him off and the more off center we can push him, the better.”

“That’s why you called him a punk, to piss him off?”

“Exactly.”

“You really think he’ll make a mistake?”

Smoke paused before answering. “How soon can you get here?”

“Two days. I need to follow up on the tracking device, confirm it’s him, and get a surveillance team together to track his movements.”

“Confirm, but don’t follow. He’s coming here that’s certain. The tracking device will tell us where he is on the island. If he spots surveillance, we’re toast. Okay?”

George calculated, then agreed. "Of course."

"Good, I'll be set up when you arrive."

"Smoke?"

"What?"

"Olivia is certain he will make a mistake?"

"She said his flaw is control. He will be vulnerable when he has to adapt to change or deal with emotion. Both will cloud his judgement." Smoke took a beat. "He has to, George. It's the only way we will get him. Lighter has too much money, too much power. If we don't get him here...now, he'll surface again, five years from now and then we won't see him coming."

"Smoke, neither one of us will let that happen. I'll call when I know something."

"Thanks." Smoke disconnected.

Felix emerged from his room in street wear. "I'm ready. David is in the lobby. Can I ask now who we're meeting or where we're going?"

They started walking to the elevator.

"Do you remember Kiki Kamealoha?"

Felix scratched his head, recalling the name from their past. "Iraq—Mosul. That was nasty business. I do remember him, of course I do. I feel like I can speak Hawaiian because I learned how to say his name. Ka-me-aloha. Right?"

"Correct, oh giant one. We are going to visit him."

"Where? I hope it's a bar. I need a beer and a burger."

"No bar."

"Okay, that's disappointing, so where are we going?"

"Wahiawa, a town in the middle of the island, up on the high plateau, near Schofield Air Field."

"A military base and no bar?"

Smoke ignored him. "Kiki asked us to meet him at a place called Healing Stone. It's kind of a shrine, I think."

"Is that weird or is it me?"

"You are as weird as it gets, buddy, but I'm a little curious. I told him why I wanted to meet and he picked the place."

"You told him why...mind telling me?"

"We know Lighter will show up here sooner or later. The story on TV told him where we're staying and we know he'll find a way here under the radar. So, we'll need eyes on this island looking for him." Smoke pushed the call button. "Do you remember him telling us Kamealoha means the beloved one? I'm hoping that's true and Kiki is connected to the local population."

Felix chuckled. "Oh, I get it. We need a... wait for it... a Lighter sighter?"

Smoke laughed loudly and pressed the lobby button on the elevator. "Now that's funny."

14

Ten days left
8:45 PM - Pacific time

When they had arrived on the island, Smoke rented a Chevy Suburban in case they needed horsepower, but he also wanted room for six and half people— Felix counted as one and a half, given his size. The choice was perfect for the highway but maneuvering the oversized vehicle on small neighborhood roads made his choice questionable. Now, driving at night to meet Kiki, on side roads, in the wide-ride vehicle, made his choice seem stupid.

Smoke eventually found the Healing Stone Shrine. It was not what the name suggested. Marble steps led to a tall well-built structure constructed with slabs of white marble. It was very small, about the size of a one-car garage. Nestled in the heart of the community, it stood between two homes and across the street from a fenced off elementary school. Healing Stone resembled more of a bus stop than a temple and appeared underwhelming as a tourist attraction.

Smoke pulled tight to the curb and he and Felix got out. They started walking toward the steps leading to the courtyard in front of the building's entrance.

"Sergeant Smoke."

Felix and Smoke wheeled around and saw their former platoon-mate, smiling, right behind them.

"You always could sneak up on me." Smoke spread his arms out.

"That's because the sniper is a sneaky bastard, Sergeant."

They embraced and Kiki turned to Felix. "Nice hair, did the guy who cut it settle out of court?"

"You know the last thing I want to do is hurt you... but it's on the list."

"You could try." Kiki put up hands, threw a fake punch at Felix's chin, grinned wide, then hugged his old friend.

The three kicked a couple of memories around for a few minutes, then the conversation got serious.

"The man we are looking for is a cruel, merciless, serial killer. He has kidnapped and murdered sixteen girls. His first victim was abducted here in Honolulu, and we know his next victim is the woman I love. She is here with me now and I am hoping that you will be able to help us."

"Of course, I'll help, but my reach doesn't go as far as—"

A set of headlights suddenly flashed on them, interrupting their conversation. An old van with faded paint and a dented fender pulled up next to them and the side panel door slid open.

A man got out. He was very big and the van shifted with the reduced weight. The giant nodded to Kiki, but didn't look at Felix or Smoke. He turned around and looked back into the van.

The big man reached to a small, old woman with long steel grey hair, wearing a purple sarong, lifting her to the sidewalk. Another woman, probably in her early twenties, wearing a similar sarong, followed. She was athletic and moved quickly to take the old woman's arm giving her support as she ambled forward. They both were obviously Hawaiian and, from their appearance, not wealthy.

The grey-haired woman walked past the three former soldiers and took the three steps up to the shrine with the young woman on her arm. The big man stayed with the van.

Smoke leaned towards Kiki. "You asked her to come here, yes?"

Kiki nodded.

"Why?"

"She is the only one who can give you what you need."

"It doesn't seem like she's going to be very cooperative."

Kiki stopped and faced the two men. "The people American's call natives have been here for almost 2,000 years. Language, culture, a way of life, which was at the center of their existence, is now a tourist attraction. If she decides to help, it won't be for you."

Kiki took the steps first. Felix and Smoke followed.

The small space was empty but for a six-sided platform,

about three feet tall. A single black smooth polished of black stone, surrounded by flowers and pieces of fruit, sat on its marble top. Leaning against the base of the platform was a framed picture of the same platform but with two stones, instead of one.

The old woman stood still, staring at the stone. A minute went by, then another. Finally, she tapped the hand of the young woman who let go of her arm and she placed a beautiful, fully bloomed yellow flower next to the onyx rock.

The old woman turned and inspected Smoke, up and down, then did the same to Felix. Her searching eyes went back to Smoke, and she stared into his for a long time. Seemingly satisfied, she broke contact, reached out, touched Kiki's arm, and nodded.

Kiki acknowledged the apparent permission to proceed with a nod. "Smoke, Felix, this is Nalani Ka'ana'ana. She is ninety-seven years old and a kanaka maoli, which means she is pure blood Hawaiian. She is also Hawaiian royalty, a direct descendant of King Kamehameha." Kiki then pointed to the young woman. "This is her great granddaughter, Makana."

Makana nodded, politely.

The old woman straightened her back and raised her chin. " 'o 'oe'ka'maka'i? "

Smoke looked at Kiki, puzzled.

"Hey man, I'm Hawaiian, but I don't speak the language."

Makana spoke. "She axed if'n ya be da policeman dats looking for da bradda man?"

Smoke, thinking he understood bradda meant bad man, nodded.

Nalani spoke. "He aha kou makemake?"

The young woman translated. "She axed, wat is it ye be wanting?'"

Smoke reached into his pocket and took out a picture of Hamilton Lighter. He held it up for the old woman to see. "I'm guessing, since I asked Kiki for help, and you're here, you can help me find this man."

Nalani looked hard at the picture than looked at her granddaughter. "O Kiki said keia no lako I lawe I ka wahine."

The young woman's head snapped around and she stared at the old woman.

The grandmother looked sternly then beckoned her to continue translating.

Tears welled in Makana's eyes. "She axed if this was da man dat tok our wahine."

Smoke nodded. "Yes, I believe he is."

The young woman had tears streaming down her face. "Da missin wahine name be Kalani Ka'ana'ana. She be my mohe kaikaina. She be my twin sister."

Nalani took a couple of steps closer to the shrine.

Smoke followed. "Why are you talking in your native tongue? I know you speak English."

"I wanted to see if Kiki was right—he was—you are very smart." The old woman looked pensive but continued. "I don't speak to Haole like you but..." she pointed to Kiki, "he is ohana, so I agreed to meet you."

She took a few more steps and then pointed to the stone. "The legend of Healing Stone is, there were two sisters from Kauai who had magical powers. Their power was great, and they would fly from island to island, healing those who needed help. But they could fly only at night. They needed to be home on their island by daybreak. One night, they got caught in the dawn's light and they dropped from the sky as stones. The stones were gathered up and put here. Our people, who still needed help, could travel here, to the sisters and ask for help." She reached up to the flower and stroked a petal. "Even after the sisters were trapped in stone, some who came were healed."

She teetered a bit and Smoke quickly supported her arm.

She smiled up at him, tears now in her eyes and patted his hand.

Smoke's voice was reverent. "Kiki has told you what I need?"

She nodded.

"Can you help us?"

Her hands rose up, palms down, as she made a sweeping gesture. "We are many, and in this, we are all ohana— family. Our eyes will watch for this man."

"Thank you."

Nalani's face now held concern. "He is dangerous, yes?"

"Very."

She shook her head. "We will help but I will not put any of our people in harm."

"No, no. There is no need for that. Tell them please, don't try to take him. I don't want anyone hurt, either. I just need to know where he is. We will take care of everything else."

She looked tired and frail, more than before. Smoke's grip on her elbow took more weight.

"Kiki said you are certain this is the man who took our wahine."

"Yes."

She turned to face him, her fingers gripped both his arms and she tried to pull him close to her face.

He let her.

She put both hands on the sides of his head, closed her eyes, then touched her head to his. "You came a great distance and now you are here asking for help. Our people will help you catch the man who took our beautiful wahine— Makana's twin sister and my great granddaughter."

"Thank you. I'll give his picture to Kiki. He will know how to get a hold of me."

She took his arm and they began walking out.

"Can I ask you a question?"

She nodded.

"There's a picture on the wall of two stones yet only one stone is here."

Nalani smiled. "There were two magical sisters transformed into healing stones. They were brought here together and many years ago, one was taken. In all my years, I have never heard of the magic helping a haole. That means—"

He grinned, "I know it means white man."

She patted his hand again and he liked it.

"The magic only works for us, for kanaka maoli. The magic has never worked for white people. But, I think, the healing stone, the sisters from Kauai, are reaching out through you to heal my granddaughter's heart. So, I give you my blessing. All will know of it and all will help. We are ohana."

Her face had deep wrinkles and her eyes became narrow. "Ino— evil— has many faces. Because you are good, you might not recognize it when it comes. If you need to call out for help, think of this place, of the sisters. Maybe the magic will help you send the ino back to Kehena. That means send him back to..."

She stopped speaking abruptly, her eyes going to the floor.

Makana stepped up. "She be too good, to be cussin'. She said send him to Kehana. That is da devil's house." Makana put her face close to his and spoke slowly. "So... tis be from me...da twin sista of the girl he killed. You, big man. You, send the ino back to... hell."

15

Eight days left
5:45 AM - Pacific time

The Falcon 7x was sixty-seven miles from Inouye International Airport in Honolulu and Captain Harry Geller was worried. Whenever his boss loaded a large parcel in the cargo hold, he usually wanted to dump it in the middle of the ocean. Mr. Lighter would give Geller the order to descend from cruising altitude, just as the plane changed radar vectors from one Air Traffic Control to another. There was always ten or fifteen minutes between New York and London or Los Angeles and Tokyo when ATC had them on their screens but didn't pay them much attention. The jet's sudden drop and quick return to cruising altitude had never been noticed.

The captain saw the usual, mysterious, plastic covered bundle being loaded into the cargo hold. It was about the same size as the other loads they had dropped, but this one had a different shape. He thought maybe the odd shape meant the load was actually going to be off-loaded in Hawaii. Somewhere inside he knew that wasn't the case. On this trip, Geller expected to be ordered to make the drop when their flight plan intersected with the Tropic of Cancer. On that latitude, the ocean was 3,000 feet deep and 1,280 miles from either city, but the order didn't come. Now, the plane was at 50,000 feet and only 250 miles from Honolulu and any fluctuation in course, altitude, or speed would be instantly detected. If Lighter ordered the dump now, Geller would have a lot to explain because the plane was in Honolulu's radar range and he was in active communication with the air traffic control tower.

The radio crackled to life. "LGN4375, this is Air Traffic Control, Honolulu. You are crossing the outer marker. Come to heading 287, descend to 30,000 feet and reduce speed to 300 knots."

"Roger, Air Control Honolulu, LGN4375 descending to 30,000 on 287 and 300 knots."

The cockpit door opened and Hamilton Lighter stepped in. "Captain, you are about to have a serious decompression issue."

"Sir?"

"I need to get into the cargo bay. Is it pressurized?"

"Yes, but if we drop suddenly it will be—?"

"It is safe to open the bay at ten thousand feet, yes?"

"Yes, but—."

Lighter cut him off again. He narrowed his eyes and spoke sharply. "Did you turn the cockpit recorder off?"

"Yes... yes, like you requested. It's off." Geller's voice was weak and compliant.

"I'm not concerned with what appears on their screens. When I'm ready, I'll use the intercom. When I signal, you will immediately notify Air Traffic Control there has been a sudden loss of cabin pressure and you are descending to 10,000 feet. After you alert them, you are to go radio silent. No more radio transmissions." Lighter lowered his voice to a growl. "Sell it, captain. You want them to believe this is an emergency, understood?"

The captain looked at Cory Watson, the copilot, who just shrugged.

Lighter grabbed the captain's shoulder his voice returning to normal. "Captain, if you pull this off, I promise you, and the entire crew, will never want for another thing for the rest of your life."

A weak smile drifted across Captain Harry Geller face.

Lighter closed the cockpit door and walked past two cabin attendants who, like the pilot and copilot, made every flight with him since he got out of the hospital/jail.

He sat down in his calf's leather recliner, picked up a

crystal glass containing what was left of his bourbon and took a sip. The liquid bit his tongue and he squinted as he swallowed the cold brown whiskey. Even though Mitchter's Sour Mash was the best on the market, the acquired taste allowing for the enjoyment of the bottle liquid fire had never come to him. He found it bitter and harsh, but he drank it anyway because it cost $3,000 a bottle.

"Would you like more ice?"

He nodded and held the glass out to Kathy Ferguson.

She had long blond hair that fell forward when she leaned over to accept his glass.

She was tall, taller than the other one, whose name he could never remember. Kathy had great legs and she always wiggled her ass when she walked away from him. He liked that. The other one, whose name he didn't care to remember, had better tits but this one had a better waggle.

Kathy returned with a new glass, new ice, and more bourbon.

Lighter pinned her fingers under his when he took the glass, his eyes flashing with sardonic pleasure. "So, have you managed to stay off the pole?"

Her jaw tightened but she recovered quickly, perhaps because her years as a stripper made her immune to assholes. "Yes sir, I have. Your generous salary is more than enough to keep me in high heels." She smiled at him then turned away, returning to the galley. She wiggled for him as expected but her face was fixed with disgust.

Lighter gazed out the oblong window in the hull. His ears were popping as the plane descended following the required landing procedure. He took another sip and picked up a cigar. The diamond and gold lighter lit with the first click. A long grey stream of smoke filled the air of the cabin. Nice Tits was preparing the cabin for landing and he smiled when he saw her face scrunch up with disapproval. He took another puff and blew it in her direction.

The engine whine changed pitch indicating it had leveled off at 30,000 feet.

He needed to move. He placed the cigar into the ashtray, got up, and walked toward the tail of the plane. A black panel on the hull held two buttons. He pressed the button marked OPEN and a hatch cover, concealed in the floor, slid toward the back of the plane. Lights went on below and he climbed down a ladder leading to the cargo hold. When he reached the floor, he pressed the CLOSE button on a panel matching the one in the cabin. The hatch slid back in place.

The space resembled a small warehouse. There were metal struts on the aluminum hull and it was colder and noisier than the cabin. He walked on a flat metal grid floor to a six-foot-long, three-foot-wide object covered with black plastic. He bent down and popped open the clasps on the restraints that strapped it to the floor. Lighter withdrew a pocketknife and slit the plastic from end to end, uncovering three backpacks.

Lighter yanked the first bag free, opened its zipper, and pulled out his new outfit. He stripped off his shoes, shirt, and pants then wriggled into a black rubber wetsuit. Reaching back into the plastic cover, he pulled out the second backpack. He put his arms through the straps, secured another across his chest, then double checked its fit by pulling the slack tight.

He walked to the hull where a microphone hung loosely from a cradle. "Where are we, captain?"

"Fifty-five miles from the tarmac."

"Good. At thirty-five miles, signal air traffic control and tell them you've lost cabin pressure then dive to 10,000 feet."

"Yes, sir."

"Are you certain the flight recorder is off?"

"Yes, sir. The recorder is off but... the black box is still recording our position."

"Don't worry about that. Use the intercom to tell the crew when you're beginning to dive. I will be able to hear you down here."

"Roger."

Lighter returned the microphone and went back to work. He reached back into the first pack and withdrew a wide, thick, canvas-covered belt, and strapped it around his waist. He opened a snap on the belt and put the pocketknife inside. He looked over at the pile of clothes on the floor and picked up his pants. Lighter felt the pockets. He started kneading the front and back pockets. Empty, he threw the pants to the floor.

"Fuck."

The captain's voice came over the intercom. "Prepare for a steep dive."

Lighter grabbed an overhead rail and spread his feet.

The plane's nose dropped sharply.

The rapid descent increased the pressure on his eardrums

causing Lighter to open his mouth and work his jaw back and forth. He had miscalculated how hard it would be to stand while the plane dropped. He struggled to get his other hand on the bar above his head, but he did, and he held on for the ninety seconds it took to get to 10,000 feet. When he let go his fingers were aching; his neck and shoulders sore from the exertion.

I need a massage.

He shook his fingers and rolled his neck. He reached up, grabbed the bar with one hand, and spread his feet again. On a second control panel, he pushed another button marked OPEN. A hydraulic motor emitted a high-pitched squeal as the cargo door began to open. Even though the pressure was equal inside and out, a rush of air blew through the compartment. Debris, loose papers, and part of the plastic covering the backpacks flew past him, disappearing into the night. The plane pitched and yawed a couple of times before it stabilized.

Lighter let go of the bar and reached into the third bag, withdrawing a small yellow square of what looked like cookie dough. He held it out, examining the black box with a red LED screen that was attached to the C4 plastic explosive.

Lighter pushed a button on the side of the box and the screen lit up. The number thirty appeared. A second later the number changed to twenty-nine.

Lighter dropped the C4 plastic explosive back into the third backpack. It landed on more cookie dough.

He walked to the end of the platform, which now was completely open, and jumped.

He fell fast for ten seconds, then he pulled the handle on his parachute. The sudden jolt stopping his fall startled him. Lighter grabbed the lines and swung his head first right then left. Pulling the right strap spun him around to where the light coming from the open cargo bay was visible in the distance.

A brilliant white flash came first, followed by a rush of air that caused his chute to spin. He struggled to turn back around, pulling hard on the straps so he could see the flaming pieces of what was left of his 80-million-dollar plane flutter as they fell to the ocean below.

It was almost as exhilarating as a kill— but not quite.

No more loose ends.

The flames died and the smoke trail went from bright white to grey.

He knew he was falling about twenty miles an hour but he felt like he was just hanging in the air. The ocean, still a mile and a half down, didn't seem to be getting any closer. Lighter looked to the edge of the horizon— to where the stars became visible above the Pacific. There were more stars than he had ever seen before, even more than when he was a teenager, burying his first kills in the empty fields in Dayton. This was amazing. From horizon to horizon, white lights twinkled against the black nothingness of space.

In the distance, he could see the glow of light from Honolulu. Looking down, he saw the ocean, which was coming up fast. He began scanning the sea, pulling on the parachute straps again, turning right and left. He stopped when he saw the green and red starboard and port lights on a boat bouncing on the water.

He felt for the handle on the wide canvas belt and yanked it hard. Instantly, a yellow plastic float burst out the seams of the canvas and the bright white LED emergency light started blinking. He angled the chute toward the oncoming boat then reached to the release handle on the parachute, preparing to hit the water.

I'm hungry.

16

Seven days left

8:45 AM - Pacific time

Smoke rolled over on his right side; eyes open, almost awake. The pain in his shoulders and back, which usually woke him up, didn't. It wasn't there yesterday, either. The injuries he had suffered in the war didn't bother him as much as they had in the past. His daily dose of pain pills had been replaced with a regime of exercise and stretching. The latter had come hard to his routine, not because it was strenuous, because it was so new-age yuppie.

O had also gently suggested, which meant insisted, on expanding his view of exercise. It went from hitting the heavy bag and running five miles to yoga and the ever-embarrassing downward dog pose. Eight months later, he no longer reached for an amber bottle of pills; now his first movement in the morning was a caress of a silk-covered thigh.

The rough skin on his fingertips dragged across the fabric of her nightgown. He listened to her breathing; not sure she was awake.

Her hips backing into him answered his question. She spooned against him, her toes pushing against the mattress, her hips wiggling away any space between their bodies.

"Morning." His voice was raspy.

"Morning." She wiggled again. "Hmmm."

He stroked her hair. She had let it grow out. The professional short, straight cut had grown shoulder length, complete with curls and bounce.

"I hope I didn't wake you." He pushed into her a bit.

"Nope, I woke up a while ago. I've just been lying here thinking how lucky I am."

He lifted his arm, up and over her shoulder, his hand coming to rest, comfortably, naturally, on her breast. They fit together perfectly, as if their bodies were built with interlocking parts. Her hips fit inside his, his knees behind hers, her head to his chin.

She wiggled again and he began rising to the occasion.

"Hmmm." She channeled Mae West, "Say there, big boy, is that a banana in your pocket or are you just glad to see me?"

"Glad no, ecstatic yes."

She reached over his hip and gabbed his butt, pulling him closer.

His hand, resting on her satin covered breast, became a caress.

"Coffee anyone?" The door to the bedroom flew open, ending the possibility of a morning rendezvous.

Smoke looked over O's head and saw the smallest bottom of a bikini ever made. Above it he saw the bottom of a tray holding two cups of coffee that covered both the view of Gia's face and Smoke's disappointment.

Gia bent over, handing a cup to O. She wasn't wearing a matching bathing suit top.

"I really don't want to be the one to tell you Gia, but there are no topless beaches in Hawaii." O took the cup.

Gia lowered the tray, handing the second cup to Smoke. He couldn't help but admire her perfect dancer's body. "That is the smallest bottom to a bikini, I think I have ever seen. Can I ask how much it cost?"

"Eighty dollars and it didn't come with a top. Now, I have nothing to wear." Gia wasn't happy when she left the room.

The mood was broken but the exchange helped O and Smoke smile through their own disappointing start of the day.

O rolled out of bed and stretched, lifting her body up and her hands to the ceiling. She raised up on her toes, her legs, her chin, her neck, every part he saw, more perfect to him than the last.

Inspired, he reached to grab her arm and pull her back to bed when his phone rang.

He grunted at the morning's second disappointment while reaching to the nightstand.

"Hello."

"Smoke, it's George. I have some incredible news. Is Olivia there?"

"Yes, I'll put you on speaker." Smoke hit the icon and laid the phone on the bed.

"As you know, we were able to intercept an email that put us onto Lighter's request to have his cigar lighter repaired. That presented an opportunity to place a small GPS device in the case of the lighter."

"That's good news. The last time we spoke your agent hadn't accomplished the plant yet." Smoke looked to O and mouthed, "Do you remember this?"

She nodded.

"He did and it was working fine. Lighter left the apartment yesterday at 7:00 p.m., New York time, then got on a jet at Teterboro airport. The flight plan had four crew members and one passenger."

"Destination?" Smoke queried.

"Honolulu, Hawaii."

"Wait. A second ago you said... it was...working. Is it or isn't it?" O asked, confused.

"Haven't gotten to that yet. Be patient. The plane took off about 8:20 eastern standard time. It stopped in Los Angeles to refuel than left for Hawaii at 11:45 pacific time. The GPS worked perfect. We were tracking it. It was sending a signal every sixty seconds."

Now, Smoke was becoming impatient and stood up from the bed. "You just said...were tracking. What's up George?"

"And then..." George continued undaunted with the interruptions, "the GPS suddenly stopped working; thirty miles short of touchdown in Hawaii."

O had confusion all over her face. "George, I don't understand. How is that good news?"

"Because it stopped working when the plane blew up."

There was silence on both ends of the transmission.

"Blew up?" whispered O in disbelief. "He's dead?"

"Yes." George was jubilant. "We don't know, why the jet exploded, yet. What we do know is the pilot reported a sudden loss of pressure at 30,000 feet. They dove to 10,000, leveled off, then suddenly boom...it blew up. The Coast Guard is on the scene but it will be weeks before we have a cause. The ocean is about 1,500 feet deep and the debris was limited to seat cushions and paper. Not much left. It'll take weeks maybe months to figure out what happened."

O looked at Smoke, still not daring to believe the news.

Smoke asked, "You sure he was onboard?"

"We have him on the security video at Teterboro. He was definitely on that plane when it took off."

Not satisfied, Smoke probed. "How about when it refueled?"

"Again, security video showed no one got off and no one got on. We also had people on the ground and they saw nothing unusual."

O's breath contained a sob. "He's dead. Really dead."

Smoke looked down to the phone. "Are you sure?"

George took a moment. "I'm as certain as I can be without a body."

"Thanks George. Stay in touch. Get me updates when you can." Smoke pushed disconnect.

O, now up on her knees, looked at Smoke then flew off the bed and jumped into his arms, her head on his shoulder, her feet off the floor. "It's over. It's finally over."

Smoke held her tight but didn't say what he was thinking.

The door opened and this time Felix ran in. "Did I just hear that fucking monster is dead?"

"Yes, you did." O dropped off Smoke, ran across the room and assumed the same off-the-floor position on Felix.

Felix spun her around and around. Her head flew back, like she was on a merry go round, and she started laughing. "Stop, stop, you'll make me throw up."

Felix returned O to earth, and still holding on said, "I know this means we can leave, but we can't, not yet."

"Why not?" O's face scrunched up.

Felix pointed to the window and the beach beyond. "Fireworks."

"Fireworks? I don't understand."

"Friday night, right by the lagoon next to the hotel, there's a huge fireworks display."

Smoke added clarity. "They used to do it every Friday night, but I understand this will be the first time since the quarantine. I saw it a couple of times years ago and it was pretty spectacular."

O's smile was glorious. She put her hands on her hips and proclaimed, "Okay it's settled then. We will stay for the fireworks and head back home on Saturday."

Cheers were heard from the other room as Gia and David joined the overture.

Smoke went with the flow but a nagging thought remained.

I'm as certain as I can be without a body.

17

Four days left
11:00 AM - Pacific time

A boat with green and red lights was surrounded by flashing red and white lights. Two Honolulu Harbor Police boats were tied off on its port and starboard. Six uniforms were examining the decks, the cabin, and the hold to determine the circumstances surrounding the murder of the crew of the *Endless Day*.

The sun was up, almost directly overhead. The uniforms were suffering in the heat and finding it difficult to perform the tedious tasks necessary to every homicide investigation. Corpse flies were buzzing over the two men near the bow. They were shot once in the head and once in the chest. The other victim, who appeared to be the captain of the ship, was the third fatality and lay half in and half out of the bridge.

"It looks professional." A uniform with three hash marks on both sleeves and scrambled eggs on his hat pointed to the two dead bodies. "One in the chest and one in the back of the head. Both shot from behind. The center mass shot came first, then double tapped with the head shot."

A uniform without the seniority was taking notes. "What about the captain?"

Sergeant Alana walked carefully to the cabin door and bent over to examine the body. "Once in the heart– not close range. I'll guess the shooter took out the crew first then shot the captain coming out the door."

Alana pointed to the photographer. "Harry, get the footprints on the deck. There's blood in them so they have to be from the shooter."

He turned to the uniform taking notes. "Did you find their wallets?"

"No wallets, sergeant, their passports were in their gear down in the cabin. They are Portuguese."

"All three?"

"Yes... I ran the hull identification number. The boat was rented out of the Keehi Harbor for a week. I got the name of the owner from the Harbor Master who told me they called him off an online ad–paid cash. They've been sleeping on it; all their belongings are below. There's cash, phones, a computer so I don't think it was a robbery. Drugs?"

"It was rented from Keehi, correct?"

"Yes."

"A local harbor, no smuggling, so it's not drugs. Anything else, Bailey?"

"There is a witness who saw the boat come into the inlet, head for the dock under control, then just turned and ran aground on the shoals at Magic Island."

"Did they hear gunshots?"

"No, but they saw flashes—thought it was a camera."

"Okay, this is good work, Bailey. Stay with this and call the airport with the names. Find out where they came from and when they landed on the island." He tapped his finger to his lips. "Also, make sure the written statements are perfect and see to it that Harry gets the photos uploaded immediately."

"Yes, Sergeant. Thank you, Sergeant." The uniform hustled off.

Alana walked to the stern and pulled out his phone. "I have to let the Feds in on this."

18

Three days left

5:00 PM - Pacific time

Smoke and O ambled along the walking trail in the park on Magic Island. A warm wind was coming off the ocean. She had her arm looped through his and their steps were matched.

The Island called Magic was actually more a peninsula, a loop of passive, quiet, and calm adjacent to the busy city. It was absolutely beautiful. Huge canopy trees stood alone on the grassy plain providing shade for small groups having a picnic, Tai Chi classes, or couples— spread out, relaxing, reading. The trees were also where some homeless souls found shelter. A juxtaposition of peace and progress.

Walking on the trail on the east side, one could watch boats coming in and out of Ala Wai Harbor, or the surfers off Kahanamoku Beach. At its point, a high rock seawall encircled and protected a lagoon from the crashing waves. The salt water cove was teaming with sea life, whose species spent millenniums developing their own wardrobes. Multicolored fish danced through the coral, like pedestrians on a sidewalk, and became a never-ending reel from nature's silent movie viewed daily by snorkelers.

The west side of Magic Island is where the Pacific runs up on a long white beach. It is also a picture-perfect beach for brides. Young princesses in white, primped and preened, are accompanied by grooms, both exhibiting endless patience, as photographers position them for one more lifetime keepsake.

"I can't remember when I've felt this relaxed." O nuzzled her head into his arm.

Smoke kept his doubts about Lighter to himself and reached to cover her hand with his.

She sighed. "I've been to Hawaii twice for conferences. I was so busy I didn't have time to do anything like this."

Smoke shook his head. "Then you really haven't seen Hawaii. I was here a couple of times... staging mostly between re-assignments in the army. But then, I stayed here after—" he had accidentally tripped over his mental block.

O looked up at him and waited for him to finish telling a secret still too difficult to talk about.

He changed course. "Real Hawaiians have a very unique feeling of family—ohana."

"It's okay, Smoke, it's okay." She turned back to the path, pulling him along.

A random ocean wave hit the wall beside them and a cool spray of water showered down from the clear blue sky.

He took her arm and hurried her further down the path, away from the crashing waves. They sat on a bench where they could watch the incoming tide build momentum. Within a minute, a huge green-headed sea turtle rose to the surface and looked around.

"My God, look at that." O squealed, pointing.

He didn't look at the turtle. He was staring at her. He stroked her cheek.

She looked up at him.

He kissed her tenderly and the warmth of her touch made the sunshine feel insufficient.

She rested her head on his chest and together the sea air purged the thoughts of the past year's troubles from their minds.

"Look there." O pointed again, this time at a young woman in a white gown walking toward the beach with her mate. He was holding her shoes and her arm. A photographer followed the pair, overloaded with camera gear.

Smoke didn't know what to say. He winced when he said, "They seem happy."

O turned to him disapproving. "Seem?"

"Well, no. I mean, I'm sure they—"

O started laughing and stuck a finger in his chest. "Gotcha."

Smoke's smile didn't crack his face. It came from the

center of his being. A rush of emotion caused a moment, a celestial occurrence. It was a pause when the energy of the universe suddenly created a single moment of clarity.

Smoke turned to face her. "Will you marry me?"

Her mouth fell open, surprised.

He couldn't believe it himself. He knew he said it, he recognized his voice.

She didn't speak. Her hands came up and covered her mouth. The pause caused the universe's energy to start to suck back into the darkness dragging along Smoke's soul.

She smiled, caressed his cheek, and spoke close to his face. "I need to know something before I answer."

He couldn't speak, so he nodded.

"I need to know what you're not telling me about Helen."

His eyes welled and he ducked his head.

She whispered into his ear. "I love you."

"I completed my first tour in Iraq and came home. I couldn't find a job after my hitch was up—" He looked at her. "Wait—that's not true. It's what I've been telling myself all these years. I re-upped because I wanted to. I thought... I made a decision that even though the separation was hard on us, we could get through another eighteen months. I convinced her that when I got back, we would be in much better shape, financially. With battle pay..." He stopped again and shook his head. "I'm justifying, again."

"What happened?"

"Helen found out she was pregnant after I had been deployed to Afghanistan. Nine months later she...we had a boy. She named him Henry."

"After you."

"Not really. You know, I hate that name, always have. We were together since high school and whenever she was mad at me, she always called me Henry. Obviously, she wasn't happy about me not being there so... Henry."

"It sounds like your relationship was very special."

"It was." He smiled a little smile.

She patted his hand, urging him on.

"Three months after he was born, my unit was pinned down by enemy fire. About fifty personnel were trapped and any minute we be could have been overrun. I was in a position to do act and I did... something any other solider would have done."

"Ah uh, and this for this 'something any solider would have done,' you were awarded the Distinguished Service Cross?"

He looked at her curiously.

"Felix told me all about you being awarded the second highest medal for valor there is— the DSC. He said the reason why you didn't get the Congressional Medal of Honor was— no one actually witnessed what you did. They only saw the results, you alive and a whole lot of dead enemy soldiers. And... in the process you saved his life, and your friend Kiki, too."

Smoke waved her off and pressed on. "I was shot up pretty bad and airlifted to South Korea. I had several surgeries and I was out of it for a long time. Eventually, I sent here to Hawaii for recovery. It took almost two years before I could get back to Philadelphia."

"You still haven't told me what happened."

"It happened the day after I got hit." His voice changed tones. It got deeper. "It was weeks before I even knew I was in Korea. Finally, I was able to ask for a phone so I could call Helen." He looked up to the sky not wanting to say the words out loud.

She remained silent like a good psychiatrist waiting for a breakthrough.

"Three men broke into our house. Helen was home with Henry. The next day, the neighbors saw the front door open and called the police. They found Helen raped and murdered..." Smoke looked up, "and Henry was gone."

He took a breath and looked down at O.

Tears were running down her face.

When he saw her crying a gusher of emotion exploded from deep inside him. He choked on his words. "If I had been there, she—" He shuddered. "Our friend, Bobby Aimer was a beat cop then but he had friends in the Police Department and I had friends who were not. Everybody was looking under every rock. When I finally got back, I looked everywhere for my son. Followed every lead, no matter how small. I've found nothing, nothing, he's gone."

Minutes passed and not a word was uttered. They just held each other.

The ocean was the only sound and its rhythm slowly brought him back to the now.

She pushed herself up off the bench, put her body in front of him, and took hold of both his hands.

Smoke became uncomfortable not knowing what to expect.

She stared at him until his eyes met hers then she knelt down, and kissed his hands one at a time. She rested her chin on his hands. "Henry Smokehouse... I've been waiting for you my whole life."

Breath came out of his mouth with the exuberance of a child. "O, I didn't know I was going to do this." He shrugged sheepishly. "I don't have a ring."

She shook her head. "You have given me way more than a silly shiny stone. You gave me your heart."

He gathered his courage and asked again. "Olivia Bennet, will you marry me?"

"Yes, Henry Smokehouse, I will marry you."

He rose up, pushing her backwards, wrapping his arms around her, and lifting her up, her face to his, her toes just touching the ground.

They came together with a kiss

19

Three days left

7:00 PM - Pacific time

Smoke decided to stay close to the hotel for a celebration dinner. O put on some pressure to have it at one of the finest restaurants in Honolulu, Le Mer, but it was at the other end of the city, near Diamond Head.

Smoke suggested instead, The Tropic at the Hilton. It had beachfront dining, music and it was near the lagoon, which would be only a short walk to the best place to view the fireworks. He pointed out this restaurant wouldn't mind a rowdy crowd as much as the one featuring exclusive fine dining.

They arrived together and were seated at a table with a view of the beach. Palm trees accented with flaming tiki gaslights illuminated the white sand and the quarter moon made the whitecaps on the ocean twinkle. To further set the stage, instead of a typical tourist show featuring ukuleles and grass skirts, a three-piece band was playing reggae with a Hawaiian/Jamaican twist. Up-tempo and fun was the music and the mood.

After they were seated, O nodded to Smoke. He took her hand and they stood together looking at their friends, then each other, all the time sporting Cheshire Cat grins.

David, Felix, and Gia looked puzzled.

O spoke first, "Smoke has an announcement."

Through a fake grin he whispered, "Chicken."

She whispered back, "Show me what you're made of, big boy."

"Grummph." Smoke cleared his throat. "Okay, right... Uhm."

Gia's face lit up. "This is big."

Felix and David looked at each other, puzzled.

"Ah... Uhmm."

"What?" Felix demanded.

"O and I have, I mean we." He sucked in a breath then ripped off the bandage. "We're getting married."

David, Felix, and Gia mobbed them. People at other tables heard the celebration and were smiling and clapping. Champagne was ordered, and fortunately, food arrived with the alcohol, temporarily forestalling over-consumption.

After dinner, Smoke pushed back a bit from the table. He had been riding a tide of emotions. He had a blush of embarrassment, which was something rare in his life, at the crew's reaction to their pending nuptials. Then there was joy, an emotion he recognized but also hadn't experienced for many years. The newish emotions were battling with apprehension, which had occupied his mind, most of time.

He sat back in his chair and looked at the faces of his friends. They were talking and laughing but he wasn't listening. The din disappeared because, at the other end of the table, he saw O, who at that moment was also looking past everyone else—her eyes fixed on his.

She smiled a knowing smile and puckered a kiss.

Breath eased from his lungs. Dread and worry, his everyday companion, dissipated like air from a balloon.

Felix's volume broke his trance.

The tension was gone from his body. His mind was relaxed and allowed the looking down and seeing of something that caused him to venture into dangerous waters. "I'm admiring your choice of footwear this evening, Felix."

Felix took the bait. "Nice huh? I just got them today." He raised a giant foot adorned with his new acquisition, bedazzled and pink. "These are slippers. Not sandals, not flip-flops, certainly not footwear, Mr. Smoke. In Hawaii, these are called slippers."

"I know what they are called. What I was wondering was—"

Felix leaned forward, grinning, "Pray tell."

"The soles on those...slippers...look like they were cut from a truck-tire but my question is where did they find a pink tire? Those are what...size 18, steel belted, all weather, snow tires, right?"

Smoke looked around. No one was laughing. They were

just staring at him.

Then together they all pointed and almost simultaneously yelled out, "He told a joke, Smoke told a joke."

"Quick, gather the womankind and children, people. The end is near," Felix bellowed.

O held up a hand. "Stop Felix, it's been a rough couple of weeks."

"Thank you." Smoke nodded to his fianceé's defense.

"It wasn't funny, but he is making the effort." Her eyes twinkled.

A new song came up from the band and Felix jumped up and grabbed O's hand for a dance.

David took Felix's empty seat next to Smoke. "So, this is really over?"

Smoke took a sip of a beer and slowly placed it on the table. "George said it right. I'm as sure as I can be with no body."

David looked pensive. "It's good though, right? We're leaving tomorrow?"

"Yeah, whatever the FBI is doing doesn't involve O being dangled as bait. So, yes we are out of here tomorrow."

David nodded and tapped Smoke's knee. "Congratulations. I'm... we, Felix and I, are so very happy for both of you."

"David, if it wasn't for you, I wouldn't be here. You saved my life when I got shot at the cabin."

David put hands on his friend and stopped him from talking. "You know what I learned here in Hawaii? Everyone has a role to play in the family. I do mine and you do yours. I think this group is just like what the Hawaiians call ohana—we are family."

Smoke looked over to Felix who now had O in one arm and Gia in the other. They were all laughing.

David shook his head. "And... every family has a crazy uncle."

When the song ended, Smoke caught Felix's attention, nodded, pointed, and then turned back to David. "I need a minute with you two."

Together, the three gathered in a hall, away from the table.

"Listen, the fireworks start in about forty-five minutes." Smoke had their attention. "Lighter is not an issue anymore, but she is a celebrity and we need to act accordingly. So, standard protection, I'll do the perimeter check. Gia will stay with O and you two take flanking positions on either side of them around the lagoon. When the fireworks are over, we escort them back to the room."

Felix looked surprised, and a little drunk. "You sure that's necessary? She hasn't been bothered by fans here."

Smoke countered, "Yes, mostly because she's been locked in her room. Let's just do our jobs. Unless of course you want to pick up the check... because if you say no then we all be off the clock—"

"Wait, No... no... good point. I guess that means the FBI is still paying for all this, right?"

Smoke smiled and walked away. He checked his watch. Twelve hours thirty-five minutes till take off and home.

20

Three days left

8:45 PM - Pacific time

Gia and O drifted along the concrete path that edged the sandy beach surrounding the lagoon. Tourists from the mainland, guests from the Hilton, and the usual laidback locals, hustled past them in pursuit of the perfect spot to view the fireworks.

A heavy woman, who was pulling a child by the hand, hip-checked O into Gia.

Gia immediately scolded her. "Hey lady, be careful."

"It's okay." O looped her arm through Gia's. "Nothing could spoil tonight."

"Of course, I'm sorry."

O tightened her hold on Gia's arm. "Isn't this just paradise?"

"It's the most beautiful place I've ever been, but then, I've never been out of the country, either. Wait... I mean I never left the United States before. No, wait, I mean—"

"I understand perfectly." O's laughter interrupted her friend and confidant. "I feel the same way. This is like another world, not another state."

Gia's smile lit up her face. "Indeed, and thanks for including me on this trip."

"Stop. You have been such a help battling against all the testosterone that surrounded me. The men are all acting like they're guarding the queen or something."

"They are," Gia said sincerely.

"Again... stop." O looked at her friend and hugged Gia's arm.

O recognized, long before this trip became necessary, how much she had leaned on Gia and Smoke after Lo was killed.

Loretta had been her office manager, assistant and advisor, bodyguard and her closest friend. She was murdered in a break-in of O's medical office. Felix enlisted Smoke who stepped up and brought justice to the men responsible, almost getting killed in the process. Somewhere along the way, quite unexpectedly, they fell in love.

Felix also enlisted Gia to help out and she fast became a friend with whom O could share her pain. Gia was vastly different than O, but her laugh was infectious and she lived a life without judgement.

Two men wearing touristy Hawaiian shirts walking toward them ogled Gia, then O.

The shorter of the two came up close. "You two looking for company? I heard these fireworks are loud and scary."

"Keep moving, bucko." Smoke appeared from behind them and caused the two men to immediately retreat.

O, still holding on to Gia, turned to Smoke. "They were harmless."

"Were... not are. Were... harmless."

O looped her free arm through his and the trio moved on. When they got halfway around the lagoon, Gia let go, running off the path to put down their beach towel.

O pulled Smoke across the sand and joined her.

Smoke surveyed Gia's selection and approved. "This is a good spot. I put Felix on station right over there." Smoke pointed to a bench along the path.

O looked and saw Felix waving. She waved back then sat down next to Gia.

Smoke got her attention back. "I positioned David at the sidewalk by the entrance to the time shares. They both will be able to see you two, providing you don't wander off."

He looked down at the two women who were looking around, not paying attention. Frowning, Smoke shook his head. "They will keep watch while you're here. I'm going to walk the perimeter. There are some open areas that—"

O's head snapped up, disappointed. "You're not staying here with us to watch the show?"

"No," he bent forward, leaning in for a kiss. "You are still who you are. It's warm and there's palm trees but this is the same as a night out in New York, Dr. O."

She held her pucker back for a second, then relented.

Smoke stood back up. "The fireworks will start pretty soon. I'll be back before the finale ends. We don't want to be caught up in the crowd when it's over, and—"

"I know, I know, and... don't wander off." O pouted.

Smoke hesitated for a second, looking at her, then walked away.

O leaned back on her arms and looked up at the sky. It seemed almost translucent. The thin crescent moon providing a nightlight was surrounded by countless sparkling stars, all on a rich, black backdrop that had dimension and depth. It was as if she could suddenly see a star behind the star.

"I'll call if we need to redeploy." Smoke's head was rotating like it was on a swivel.

"No worries, buddy." Felix put a hand on his shoulder to get Smoke's attention. "This is a no brainer. Look at the crowd. It's moms and pops, kids, honeymooners. Come on man, relax."

"I'll relax when we get back to New York. I'll tell David to move up after the fireworks start."

"Where are you going to be?"

"There's high ground on a ramp where I can see the whole lagoon. Like I said, I'll call you if I need you."

"I got ya."

The beach filled in a bit more, and conversations from the gathering crowd broke her concentration. A red light appeared in the distance; she saw the shadows of a crew, readying the fireworks, just off the harbor near the ocean.

O shifted around on the towel, suddenly uncomfortable. "Damn it."

"What's up?" Gia asked.

"I have to pee."

"Smoke told me the show is put on as a promotion by the Hilton and only lasts about twenty minutes. Can you hold it that long? If we run back to the hotel now, we might miss it."

O gritted her teeth. "I definitely don't want to miss the show. I can do it but only if it starts soon."

A short but powerful whoosh grabbed their attention. High in the sky, a white flash was followed, a nanosecond later, by a thunderous boom, ending the peace on the beach. A second, then a third explosion had everybody looking up.

A series of whooshes followed behind the opening salvo. Umbrellas of pink, red, and yellow drifted down, then were replaced with whistling streamers of silver. Some rockets reached their apex and popped delicately, releasing almost silent bursts of color. Others were more violent, echoing off the hotels. Rocket after rocket launched, each a new dancer on the night sky.

The first rocket launched as Smoke reached the ramp. Its explosion echoed off the glass and steel building. Suppressing his bad feeling was getting more and more difficult.

Smoke walked up the short incline, found an observation post, and scanned the crowd. Everyone was standing still with their eyes trained on the sky. Out of the corner of his eye, he saw a man in his twenties, wearing a red baseball cap, moving slowly through the crowd. He was definitely not there for the show. Smoke quickly searched the rest of the lagoon.

Fuck.

The redheaded TV reporter, with a cameraman and a soundman in tow, was walking along the path. She was talking on her phone. Smoke looked back to the red baseball cap. He was talking on his phone.

Smoke hit Felix's number. "We have incoming at your 12 o'clock. That TV reporter and a crew are moving east toward you and O. There is a scout with a red baseball cap in the crowd looking for O. It will take about three minutes for me to get there. Head west and stop her from getting closer. Call David. He can come up on them on their six."

"Roger that."

Smoke saw Felix start to move. He couldn't see David, but had confidence he would get there. He ran down the ramp and darted across the sand to the back edge of the trail.

O watched through eyes filled with amazement and discomfort. Finally, she jumped up. "Damn it. I can't hold it. I have to pee."

Gia immediately grabbed up the towel. "Let's hit it. We'll get Felix on the way back to the hotel."

They hustled back to the path, picking their way through the crowd. The park bench where Felix waved was empty.

A mother holding a child's hand heading back into the crowd was walking toward them. "Bathroom? She couldn't wait either. Over there." She pointed to a spot-a -pot.

O smiled. "Oh, thank you. You're a lifesaver."

A blue portable toilet was just outside the gate, near the parking lot. O gritted her teeth. "I hate those things but I'm not going to miss the finale."

Gia stayed right behind O but couldn't help looking over her shoulder at the fireworks.

When they reached the gate, O turned to Gia. "Wait here. Watch the show. I'll just be a minute."

O took ten quick steps then opened the door to the portable john. She sniffed and shook her head, but determined, she went in. She dropped her shorts and squatted over the opening.

Felix had the TV cameraman by the collar and the redhead was assaulting him with her microphone. "Lady, I haven't ever hit a woman but I am seriously tempted to break that streak."

Smoke had come up across the beach and arrived in time to stave off Felix's potential felony assault.

"You're not getting any closer to Dr. Bennet than this."

The redhead beckoned to the cameraman to roll camera, to which Felix made an adjustment on the man's collar convincing him that was a bad idea.

"What do you want?" Smoke asked.

"I need a statement on Hamilton Lighter's death. He was obviously following her to Honolulu when his plane blew up. I have a source inside the FBI who told me Lighter was a suspect in multiple murders, including Dr. Bennet's sister. Is that true?"

Smoke remained silent but had a little more respect for her detailed research.

"I just need a minute of tape. A one-line statement."

After mulling it over, Smoke offered a deal. "One question that I approve. It will receive a very short answer that you will broadcast in its entirety. No creative editing."

"Deal." The reporter grinned.

"Not yet." Smoke held up a stop sign hand. "You have to tell me how you found out she was going to be here."

The redhead lifted her head defiantly. "I don't reveal sources."

Smoke folded his arms.

Rockets were firing off and exploding over their heads.

She tapped her foot and then blurted out, "Okay, okay. I got a call from one of the wait staff. I've been trying to get info on her from the hotel staff all week with no luck. Then tonight right before I did a live update, a waitress in the restaurant called and said she overheard your plans for tonight."

He unfolded his arms. "Okay." Smoke nodded to Felix who let go of the cameraman's collar.

David came up from behind the crew. "I'm here."

Felix shook his head, "Too late, you missed the fireworks."

"Funny, very funny." David shook his head and followed as the group began walking toward where they left Gia and O.

A roar from the crowd echoed inside the smelly, blue plastic toilet as a multitude of rockets were fired off, signaling the finale.

Whoosh, whoosh, whoosh.

One after another, the rockets went up. The multicolored streamers and deafening explosions were followed by a symphony of *oohs and ahhs.*

"Damn it." O finished as quickly as she could. Looking down, still buttoning her shorts, she used her hip to push open the door.

She took half a step and looked up— right into the face of Hamilton Lighter.

"Oh my God."

He was on her in an instant, pushing her back into the darkness.

The last thing she felt was the needle he stabbed into her neck.

21

Three days left

11:45 PM - Pacific time

There was a group of people around FBI supervisor George DiSanto. Some wore uniforms, some suits and ties, all were attentive and silent. He was instructing them on how he wanted the search for Doctor Oliva Bennet conducted.

Smoke was not with them. He stood alone near the gate where O was last seen. Crime scene tape stretched from the beach to the parking lot and then across the road from the port-a- john. A forensic team was dusting the plastic door, looking for DNA and putting anything and everything in plastic bags marked EVIDENCE. A photographer was exhausting his camera's flash battery.

Also not present at the briefing was Felix. He was standing slightly behind Smoke.

Without turning around Smoke asked, "How's Gia?"

"David is with her."

"I asked how she was."

"She was hysterical at first but David got her to calm down a bit."

"Did she see what happened?"

"No. O told her she had to go to the bathroom and the hotel was too far so they went to use the port-a-pot. Gia went with her but O made her stay at the gate, so she could watch the fireworks. She was about where you are now. She couldn't see the door to the toilet."

"Then what?"

"Gia said that there was a lot of noise when the finale started. After a couple of minutes, she got concerned and went to check on her, but when she got there, O was gone."

Neither man spoke— there was nothing left to say.

Smoke turned around. "George told me it was Lighter."

Felix gasped. "What?"

George walked up to them. "An island-wide alert has been issued. Every TV and radio station are broadcasting an 800-contact number and her picture. We have the complete cooperation of HPD, our local FBI office, and fifteen agents from California are on a plane as we speak."

"How did we not know he was alive?" Smoke's tone was controlled but menacing.

George's voice reflected his guilt. "We should have. The local PD reported to our office that three bodies, all homicides, were found on a day-rental boat yesterday about noon. Our agents dug in and got IDs. They were Venezuelan, arrived a week ago but that's as far as they got. Then tonight, around seven, the HPD informed us a wetsuit was found near where the rental boat went up on the rocks. That in itself wasn't much but they said they also found a flotation collar with an LED emergency signal device attached to the wetsuit."

Smoke's eyes were wide and fixed.

"Lighter must have parachuted, and the boat must have been there to pick him up. I believe, now, he began planning to blow up the plane as soon as you left for Hawaii. He arranged for a boat to pick him up and then murdered the crew. It was all part of a bigger plan. A plan where he kills four crew members and the three men on the boat. I also think, it is more than possible, he didn't even know we planted the bug in his lighter. That was something that we thought gave us an advantage but actually helped to give him more time. He made us believe he was dead so we would drop our guard."

"But how did he know when to try to take her?"

Felix stepped to Smoke's shoulder. "We weren't watching TV."

Smoke flared. "What?"

"That TV reporter, Diane Copula, just told me she did a remote for the five o'clock news that was on the local station updating the investigation of the plane crash. During the broadcast she mentioned that O was staying in Hawaii to watch the fireworks tonight."

Smoke kicked at the dirt as George gave his theory. "Lighter was in the parking lot where he could see most of the lagoon. We would have seen him sitting in a car, so it is most likely he was in a panel van with blacked out glass in the side door."

"Right." George motioned to an agent who immediately ran up from the sidewalk. "Get the video from every camera in the area. Check with those condo buildings and get whatever security footage they have. If anybody gives you a hard time about a subpoena call me immediately. You're looking for a..." He turned to Smoke.

"An old panel van, six to ten years old. It would be a local contractor or delivery vehicle. It will have a black glass panel in the side door and reported stolen two days ago."

George added, "Also, get the footage from transit. Check for that vehicle coming or going after 7:00 p.m."

George tried to comfort him. "This isn't on you."

"Yes, it is."

Smoke turned away and he and Felix left George to his crew.

Felix broke the silence. "What next?"

Smoke took a beat. "He will follow the pattern he used with the others. If we don't find her by midnight tomorrow, he'll kill her."

"We're going to find her." Felix tried to be strong.

Smoke nodded. "Only if we get help." He took out his phone and hit a redial button.

Kiki answered his call on the first ring. "I just heard on the news. Is it true? Lighter kidnapped your girl?"

"I need to meet with Nalani. She's the only one who can keep her alive. Can you make that happen?"

"Just tell me when and where."

"Wherever she wants and as soon as possible."

"I'll call you right back."

His phone rang before they got back to the hotel.

"Are you at the Hilton?"

"Yes."

"We'll be there in twenty minutes. We'll meet you in the lobby of the Ali'i."

Kiki came in first followed by the same giant man who was at the shrine. Nalani Ka'ana'anaa came in last.

When the concierge saw her, he immediately came out from behind the desk. "It is an honor to have you visit us, Kupunawahine. How can I be of service?"

"Thank you, my child, but I am here to speak to this gentleman."

"Thank you for coming." Smoke gestured to an unoccupied space with a couch and chairs.

She nodded. "Kiki told me of your trouble. I will do whatever I can to help."

"Thank you."

She sat on a chair. "What do you want me to do?"

He knelt on one knee in front of her. "I know you have the man's picture but he is too smart to be seen in public. I need you to reach out to anyone who might have recently rented a house or apartment that is off the grid, someplace remote but secure and probably expensive. Ask if anyone has delivered food or a package that had no name, only an address. It would have been someplace where there didn't seem to be anyone home."

She nodded again. "I can do that."

"This is very time sensitive. If we don't find her by midnight tomorrow, he'll kill her."

She stood and took his arm, gesturing him toward the door. "What will you do when you get him?"

His jaw clenched and his eyes narrowed.

Her expression told him she knew.

She stood there; her face as grim as his. "Will you do something for me?"

"Name it."

She pulled his arm down and he bent over. She whispered in his ear.

He stood up, surprised.

She patted his hand and started walking to the exit. "Don't forget, now, if you need the sisters, they will be there."

She beckoned to the big man and the two left the lobby.

22

Last day
2:15 PM - Pacific time

Twenty-five men and women were crowded into a room in the FBI field office meant to accommodate far fewer people. The room was buzzing with fast paced activity and loud conversation.

Felix and David were sitting in front of monitors watching what seemed like endless hours of video from the security cameras. The Hawaiian police collected video recordings from every available source. They were scouring film from traffic cameras, ATM machines, and building security videos, looking for an old panel van with a black glass panel in the side door, anywhere near Magic Island.

A team of HPD personnel poured over traffic tickets, parking tickets, and stolen car reports. Their hunt was hampered because it was Sunday and if a delivery or construction vehicle was stolen on Friday night it might not be reported till Monday morning.

Eight FBI agents, seated together at a long table, had expanded their search for a house Lighter might have rented to include a warehouse, storage garage, or a house trailer.

Another team of FBI agents were tracking down every boat rental or private boat arriving on the island.

Smoke and George were sitting opposite each other, at an empty table. Both were oblivious to the commotion.

Smoke drummed his fingers on the table. "I have to start at the beginning, again."

"Okay," George nodded, "ten times a charm."

Smoke shot him a look. "We are concentrating on finding the vehicle but we haven't thought about how he got out without being seen." He pointed to a white board filled with information pinned and identified with black markers. "Can we put a street map and surrounding area up there?"

"Of course." George instructed an agent who seemed to be the second in command. "Agent McMahon, put up an area map of the harbor, hotels, and surrounding streets on the board."

Smoke waited with his head down, able to concentrate in spite of the racket.

Once the map was up, Smoke stood and examined it carefully. When finished, he turned and asked McMahon, "Do you have a blow up of the lot?"

"Yes sir."

George gestured to a couple of curious agents who had gathered around to back off, then turned to Smoke. "What are you thinking?"

Smoke put his hand to his chin scratching the stubble on his chin. "Agent, can you outline, the limits of the all of the security cameras ranges on the map of the lot and the entrance?"

"Yes sir," Agent McMahon responded, then solicited another agent to assist.

After several minutes of collaboration and comparisons, the extent of several all of the cameras angles were marked in black arcs on the maps.

Smoke examined the new information carefully then pointed to a few spaces near the gate. "We now know he didn't park the van the day of, so he had to have parked it there the day before— on Thursday." He pointed to an area outside of the arcs. "Look at these angles. It's easy to see that this area, right across from the toilets, wouldn't be covered by surveillance cameras. He probably was in the van for both days waiting for an opportunity."

McMahon seemed unconvinced. "Really? Seems like a real long shot that she would walk right by there."

Smoke accepted the criticism. "Maybe, but if you were familiar with the area, you would know the shortest way to get to the park, without going all the way out and around the hotel, is along this path near the lagoon."

He turned to George, his face drawn and sullen. "This is why it's on me, George. I should have seen this bottleneck.

Every guest in the hotel eventually walks out that gate, past the harbor and out to the sidewalk leading to Magic Island. I should have fucking seen this."

"You were protecting her from TV crew, Smoke." George put his hand on Smoke's shoulder. "You didn't know Lighter was still out there. Nobody knew."

George then turned to the agent. "Get a team looking at the film from Thursday."

The agent hustled off and George turned back to Smoke. "Okay, you established how he got in but how did he get out without showing up on a camera?"

Smoke took his thinking position, pacing, deep in thought. He studied the map, moving back and forth over the same path over and over again.

George took a seat and watched him work.

"Got it. I got the van." An excited voice from the table near the door rose above the noise.

George snapped to attention and walked to the Agent, but Smoke's focus was on the map.

George hustled across the room. A brown panel van with a window in the side panel rolled past the camera. "That's it."

The agent tapped the screen. "The van passed the ticket dispenser at 9:45 a.m., Friday. The space number is entered into the machine and a ticket was dispensed at 9:50."

George tapped the agent's shoulder. "Did anyone look for expired parking in the lot?"

"No sir, I don't believe so."

"Get on it. There might be a parking violation with a plate number."

The agent lowered his voice. "Sir, how did Smoke know the van was old? I get the blackout panel window but why not a new van?"

"Easier to steal. Anything made in the past five years is difficult to steal without special equipment. And don't forget about GPS tracking on company vehicles. If a battery is charged, a stolen vehicle can be found."

"Ah." The agent hit the play button on the camera from the ticket dispenser.

"There he is."

The image of a man wearing a hoodie and a black Covid mask appeared on the screen. He put in cash and a ticket for a parking spot was issued. The only facial feature visible were his eyes. The man took the ticket, looked directly into the lens, then walked away.

George leaned in. "That's him."

George walked back to Smoke who was standing, facing the white board.

"He jumped the curb to get out." Smoke pointed to where the driveway exiting the lot ran alongside a maintenance road. "Look, he jumped it here, then got out onto Kalakuaua Blvd. through the Hilton parking lot."

George yelled instructions to another agent.

Smoke shook his head. "It doesn't matter how he got out. He's ditched the van by now, anyway. My bet is you'll find it in a ravine in a day or two." Smoke looked at his watch. "We have less than ten hours."

The air was hot and thick and reeked of mold. O's head hung down, chin on her chest. Water dripping from a pipe near the ceiling hit the top of her head— after hours of being suspended in the air, every drop hit like a punch.

Sweat streamed down her forehead, ran across her cheek, and trickled off her lips. She couldn't wipe it off because her hands were tied behind her back. O's feet were spread shoulder width apart with a metal bar and secured with duct tape. Her footing was wobbly because she was standing on a small wobbly stool. Around her neck was a noose. Lighter strung a rope over a pipe in the ceiling. When the muscle fatigue from balancing on the stool forced an involuntarily jerk, the rope tightened, cutting off her air supply.

O shook her head; her hair flinging the sweat from her face. It was becoming more and more difficult not to show fear, which she knew was her only defense.

She heard the sound of distant waves become louder. It announced the opening of a door somewhere outside this chamber of horrors. She heard it before. He would be coming. Bile from her stomach erupted into her mouth and she gagged.

Her eyes narrowed and she lifted her chin, spit, and gritted her teeth.

The door opened and Hamilton Lighter hit a light switch.

O's eyes blinked hard and she rocked a bit on the stool; the rope instantly caused her to choke.

"Careful. I would hate to have this end... prematurely."

"Fuck you." O's voice was weak and cracked badly.

Hamilton grinned and approached her slowly. "Look at

you, all defiant in the face of your inevitable, painful, death. Don't you know, it's all so... so... useless."

"Fuck... you."

"Oh, that is so unladylike, Olivia, but... I have to admit, you're tougher than I thought you'd be. I mean with all the star treatment you've received, I imagined you'd be soft and begging for mercy by now." He pulled an ivory handled pocketknife from his pants pocket. "Soon, I will tell you the whole story—start to finish. I'll tell you step by step, how I came up with the plan to pay you back for the years you took from me. But... that will have to wait, because..."

He took the point of his knife and held it up to her face, then pricked her shoulder with the point like he was testing meat in an oven. "Nope, not quite done yet."

A small trickle of blood oozed out of the wound.

"I will say this, there were only two others who lasted as long as you have before they started to cry and beg for mercy." He flipped the blade open and closed as he strutted. "There was a hooker— and she was more nasty than tough— always cursing. She fought me right up to the end."

He dragged a metal chair over and straddled it backwards, facing her.

"The other defiant one was the very first sister I killed." He grinned and moved his head around trying to get O to look at him. "She was also the most fun...up to now, that is. She was a Hawaiian girl." He stretched his arms out and grinned. "I killed her... right here, in this room. Exactly where you are, right now."

Her stomach clenched and yellow fluid spilled from her

mouth. The sudden movement tightened the noose but O summoned strength and regained her footing.

He laughed loudly. "Yes, now that's much better. It looks like I'm finally getting to you."

He stood up, stepped back, and put his hands on his hips. "I didn't expect to be back here again. It's kinda' weird, when I think about it. This place originally belonged to a tech mogul who was rich for a while, then wasn't. He spent a fortune building this fortress into the side of a mountain and then lost it overnight when his computer app had an epic failure. I had originally planned to kill you at a property I found in upstate New York. It was perfect, secluded and secure, just like this... but, then out of the blue, you fly away." He stood up and flashed his knife again. "And irony of irony you and your posse came... to the scene of the very first sister, right here... in paradise. It just couldn't be more perfect for me. The perfect ending to my perfect plan."

He stood in front of O, his legs spread and chest out. "That Hawaiian girl—she didn't curse, didn't cry. She just took whatever I dished out but," he balanced the knifepoint on a finger maneuvering his hand to keep it from falling. "But... she was my first and there is a learning curve." The knife fell. He caught it before it hit the floor. He got close to her ear and whispered. "I got much better."

He took a step back and used the blade to cut the buttons off her blouse.

She fought the panic.

He ran the knife point down to the center band between

the cups of her bra. He slipped the blade under the elastic and pulled it out. He looked into her eyes.

She gave him nothing.

Suddenly, Lighter pulled the blade out and the elastic snapped back against her chest.

He kicked the metal chair over as he stepped back, the sound rattling off the walls. "When I come back, we are going to have a long chat about how I killed your sister."

He walked to where the rope was tied to a hook in the wall, gripped and pulled.

O's head slanted violently, the rope lifting her up onto her toes.

She gasped hard for air that wasn't there.

He used a free hand to unloop the rope from its hook then let it go. The rope went slack. Helpless, O fell from the stool. Her right foot hit first followed by her shoulder. Her head hit last, bouncing off the concrete floor.

Everything went black.

23

Last day

5:48 PM - Pacific time

The room was quiet because the enthusiastic banter of the agents diminished as the possibility of uncovering the whereabouts of Hamilton Lighter faded. They were almost shoulder to shoulder pouring over every possibility yet coming up dry, and their silence reflected that Dr. Bennet's time was running out.

Smoke, Felix, David, and George had gathered to refocus their efforts.

George was updating progress. "So far, we have the vehicle on video coming out of the hotel parking lot and then heading east on Kalakuaua Blvd. Lighter then drives downtown where we lose track of the vehicle when he drives in the residential section, near the zoo. The teams then looked at every camera on Highway 1, but saw nothing. Lighter had to have taken the backroads out of Honolulu." George sighed with disgust. "He could be on either side of the island or a just a mile away in the high-rise."

"Definitely not a high-rise." Smoke shook his head showing his frustration. "He's remote, off the grid. It's isolated, and deserted."

George responded, "We know, we know, Smoke, we're looking everywhere."

Smoke raised his voice. "Then we need to look again."

Felix stepped in front of Smoke. "Okay, you need a break. Let's take a walk."

Smoke shook him off, "No. I'm not leaving. We have to find her."

"I wasn't asking. You're taking a walk." Both of his paws went to Smoke's shoulders and he spun him around and guided him towards the door.

The air outside the FBI's office was cool and smelled much better than the close quarter perspiration pit they had been working in for the past eight hours.

Felix leaned against the wall and sighed. "Damn, I wish I still smoked."

Smoke paced; his present and past were being mashed together and were rumbling in the bowels of his being.

"You goin' to be okay?"

Smoke looked at Felix. "Only if I get her back. If I don't, I..."

Felix remained quiet.

"I can see her terror. I can...feel her pain."

"I know."

"When I find this guy...I swear to God—"

The front door swung open and George came flying out. "We got something."

Lighter looked into the broken mirror hanging on the bedroom wall. He smoothed the fabric over the buttons on the silk shirt then made half a turn to look at the crease in his pants. Satisfied he picked up a hair brush and combed back his jet-black hair.

He leaned over and looked closely at his profile. "Hmmm." He pulled the skin below his eyes. "It'll definitely make me look younger."

He leaned back and thought about his new identify. He had decided on higher cheek bones and a more roman nose but wasn't sure about changing his chin. He turned sideways, right then left, keeping his eye on his profile. "Hmmm."

Younger fa sure.

It was nothing he had to decide right now anyway. There was plenty of time. He could plot his next masterpiece of death, after he inflicted the maximum amount of pain on Olivia Bennet.

There was a moment when he was almost grateful to her because he had learned so much about how to be successful at executing his passion in the hospital. The hospital staff were careful to keep another man with a similar predilection away from him. What they didn't know was two other patients, receiving treatment for schizophrenia and bipolar disorder, were also serial killers. Lighter got quite an education on how not to get caught. He had learned a lot and was now preparing to disappear into the shadows and gorge himself on life's excesses and pleasures. He would recede from the spotlight and the attention of law enforcement until he felt the need to emerge from the dark to prey on the next set of the weak and helpless.

He walked to the balcony sliding glass doors and pushed them open and took in a lungful of air. "Ahhh."

He looked as his watch and rubbed his hands together. "Time for some more fun."

Lighter walked along the balcony that connected several rooms of the house. The first room was small and had a wall of monitors focused on the driveway entrance, the front door, and on the property on either side of the house. The next room was empty as was the next but the last had stairs leading down under the house. At the bottom was a concrete block room where an electric backup generator and Dr. Oliva Bennet were stored.

Lighter pushed open the metal door and saw she was still where he left her—face down on the floor.

He approached cautiously. "Olivia." He sing-songed her name. "Wakey, wakey." He poked a toe into her side.

She didn't move.

A little frustrated, he poked her again, harder. "Don't make me mad, Dr. Bennet. Wake, the fuck, up." He kicked her again, harder.

She screamed.

"Ah... there you are."

He stepped over her, bent down, and picked her up. He lifted her up on the stool, the noose around her neck slack. "See, that wasn't so bad, was it?"

"Fuck...you."

"Tisk, tisk. That's no way for a lady to talk." Lighter walked back to the wall by the door and picked up the rope. "You really need to expand your vocabulary."

He looked at her with wide eyes, a cruel smile appearing with a thought. He paused, anticipating the moment, then yanked hard on the rope.

Her neck bent sideways— the rope choking off any sound.

He let it slack then yanked again.

She struggled to remain still but it was almost impossible. Blood from where her head hit the floor dried on her forehead and her left eye was swollen closed.

Lighter adjusted the tension on the rope so she could plant her feet flat.

She caught her breath. "I can't do this."

"Olivia, you have to do this because you are completely alone."

O's head was tilted slightly and her legs shook.

He came up on her good eye. "Of course, if you say please... no pretty please—."

"Pretty please... go fuck yourself."

"Oh, now that's disappointing. Oh well, I'm going to go eat because I'm hungry. When I come back, we will have a conversation I know you're just dying to hear—all about how I killed your sister."

He opened the door still chuckling, and turned off the light.

From the dark he heard her whisper, "Smoke, where are you?"

George ran ahead, stopping when he got to a table that held the phone conferencing device. He hit the blinking button. "Harry?"

"I'm here."

"Smoke, Felix, this is Harry Serpico, our forensic computer analysis expert. Harry has found something important. Go ahead, Harry."

"Right. I have been breaking down the code to the encrypted email Lighter was using in New York."

"You found him?" George sounded surprised.

"No, not exactly."

"What does that mean?" Smoke questioned.

"We intercepted an encrypted email about a lighter that needed repair which was sent to an address. I found the address of the computer that received the emails but I didn't know who sent it. But I knew if I found who sent the email, we could find whomever was helping Lighter. If we found them, we would be able to find Lighter, because the person who sent the email is most likely continuing to support him."

George was impatient. "Harry, can you cut to the chase here. We are running out of time."

"Sorry, of course. I broke the IP address about a half hour ago and I now know who sent the email."

"Terrific, I'll call a judge and get a warrant and I'll call the section chief and he'll mobilize a team to—"

"Ah...George."

"What?"

"Are you alone?"

"Why?"

"Well I kind of went ahead and—"

"Harry, I get it, we'll fix whatever you did later. What did you find out?"

"The email belongs to Angela Bower. She lives in Tucson, Arizona. She is Lighter's

assistant and arranges for everything from cash deliveries to sheets on the bed. But..."

"But what? Jesus H Freecking Christ, will you just break it down." George's blood pressure was causing the veins on his temple to pulsate.

"Sorry, she arranged for $25,000 in cash along with clothes and food to be delivered to 1567 Waialua Ranch Road. It's an old abandoned pineapple processing plant outside of the city of Waialua. I did a search and found out there are five buildings on the property all of which have operating electric and water service. I'm still looking for a connection for that property to any of Lighters companies, but so far no joy."

Special agent McMahon had come up on the group. "Confirm the address."

Harry answered quickly. "1567 Waialua Ranch Road,

Waialua."

George spun on his heels and commanded McMahon. "Assemble your team and be ready to move in ten."

Felix stood up. "Hey, what's going on?"

Smoke looked at George. "Are we invited to this party?"

"I'm sorry, but you cannot participate in the capture. You're civilians. You can't even carry a gun in this state. But even more than that, you are personally connected to Olivia. If Lighter gets a paper cut in the arrest, his attorneys will have a field day. Do you really want that?"

Smoke's jaw was clenched but he held back his anger. He looked to McMahon. "Are you familiar with the area Serpico was talking about?"

"Yes, North Island, very remote."

Smoke touched George's shoulder. "Are you going with them?"

"Me, no." George relaxed a little. "I'm too old. I'll just get in the way."

Felix started to object but Smoke waved him off.

The agents in the room abandoned their computer screens to ready their weapons.

George shouted to McMahon, "I'll alert the Honolulu Police SWAT team that you will lead the team and coordinate with HPD."

The room emptied quickly.

George walked away.

Smoke motioned to Felix and David and the three gathered at an empty table.

Smoke saw George on the phone in his office. "It doesn't sound right to me."

Felix scratched his head, confused. "What, you think she's not there?"

Smoke didn't respond. They were standing in an office that was now deathly quiet. Panic began pulsating in Smoke's ears.

"Smoke." Felix prompted him to continue his reasoning.

"I think Lighter is playing us. It's another chess move. He anticipated we would find his assistant and the pineapple plant. I think it's a red herring. He wants to distract the police to give him more time."

Felix jumped in. "Shouldn't we tell George? Maybe he'll redirect his—"

Smoke shook his head. "He won't. They have to act on this solid evidence. His whole team will be chasing the wind."

David looked puzzled and worried. "I get it but that leaves just us. We have no clues— no FBI, no police, no helicopters. How are we going to find her?"

"There's a way... but we'll have to be ready to move quickly. She could be anywhere on the island." Smoke checked his watch. "We have to get to her before midnight—four hours and ten minutes."

Smoke reached for his phone.

24

Last day

7:39 PM - Pacific time

One hour and twelve minutes after leaving the office, Special Agent McMahon was sitting in a mobile command post in a Safeway shopping center parking lot, a mile from the pineapple plant.

Honolulu SWAT supplied a vehicle used to coordinate their remote tactical missions. It was equipped with every method of communication imaginable including a live feed to FBI headquarters in Honolulu.

SWAT was handling assault and capture, while HPD handled the traffic grid and roadblocks.

The FBI, specifically McMahon, was in command and was following George DiSanto's crystal clear orders.

Rescuing Doctor Olivia Bennet was priority number one.

Capturing Hamilton Lighter, alive or dead, was number two, but McMahon knew if Lighter somehow managed to escape, it would be his ass.

The pineapple processing facility had five buildings on the property. The first three were long low warehouse structures that had large open spaces and small mechanical rooms.

It took thirty-five minutes for two SWAT teams to clear them.

The two remaining buildings were more problematic. The first was a one-story office building that had a lot of small rooms to search. The second was a century-old, two-story farmhouse.

They were built close to each other and police going in through front or back doors would be easily spotted from any window.

McMahon studied the problem and decided on clearing the office building first.

He sent Alpha team in through a window on the blind side of the building. It was time consuming and took the team more than twenty minutes to give the all-clear signal.

The last building was the family farmhouse. It was in the very back of the property and the last in the search process.

Even though McMahon thought it was the most likely building to contain Lighter's lair, it was the last they could reach without being seen.

George DiSanto's voice came through a speaker. "Special Agent McMahon, what is the hold up? It's been almost two hours and you still haven't cleared all the buildings."

McMahon ducked his head and whispered, "Jesus Christ."

The agent monitoring the screens handed McMahon a microphone.

McMahon pressed the mic's talk button. "Happening right now, sir. Will advise." He threw the mic to the desk and put on a radio headset. "Team leader Alpha, you are clear for entry. Team leader Beta, follow after Alpha issues the go command. Report any contact, immediately."

A hissing sound crackled, "Alpha command, roger that."

Another hiss followed immediately, "Beta command, roger."

McMahon turned to another agent who was controlling the images on the monitors and pointed to the center screen. "Can you clean up this image?"

McMahon saw Alpha team's four officers lined up, single file against the wall. A bulky man in front of the line carried a metal battering ram.

On the upper screen, Beta team was lined up waiting by a door at the rear of the building.

"What's he waiting for?"

"Weapons check, sir—mandatory."

"Damn, that should have been..." He took a breath. "It's taking too long."

Seconds ticked by as Alpha team continued to ready, then the speaker rattled, "Go, Go, Go."

The bulky man slammed the ram into the door. Alpha team rushed past him into the darkness.

The upper screen showed Beta team mirroring effort.

George DiSanto was staring at the action being live-streamed from the pineapple plant to his FBI office.

"Agent, put Alpha team's body cams on screen one and Beta on two."

The agent keyed in the commands and shadowy forms, highlighted by their green night vision cameras, appeared on the monitors.

The men were methodical, moving slowly down a long hall then up a set of stairs to the second floor.

Alpha leader reported in. "No movement, no sound."

Smoke looked at Felix and David then nodded toward the door of the office.

A radio crackled. "We have movement."

The three stopped and turned back to the screens.

The pause of a few seconds seemed like a few minutes.

Beta team had halted at the top of the stairs.

"Sounds coming from end of the hall." The green image of the Beta leader moved forward.

George was riveted to the screen.

The Beta leader came to the last door and made hand signals to the men following behind him. He held up four fingers, then folded one at a time.

The door splintered when the ram hit it. The team went into the room fast.

The image on the screen blurred but when it stabilized it only took a second to recognize the squad of police had weapon superiority over a resident family of mongoose.

"Damn." George picked up a mic. "McMahon."

"Yes, sir."

"Send both teams to canvas the property. Maybe there's an underground structure somewhere we don't know about."

George knew he was grasping at straws but continued to stare at the screens.

He didn't notice Smoke, David, and Felix walking out the door.

"I was hoping I was wrong, but now we know, she's not there." Smoke slumped against the wall in the hall.

"What about the call you made? Anything?"

David looked at Felix puzzled. "What call?"

"Smoke called Kiki."

"How come?" David looked at Smoke.

"Something the tech guy, Serpico, said might be the way to find her."

Felix smiled at David. "Wait for it, this is good."

"Serpico said Lighter's assistant had packages delivered to the pineapple plantation, remember?"

David nodded. "Sure, he said there were three, all small and all addressed to Harold Shipman. It said to leave them in the mailbox at the entrance to the property."

"George told us that was the name Lighter used at the apartment he rented in New York."

"I remember... the email to fix the watch for Harold Shipman."

"Exactly. Well, we just watched two teams go through five buildings. There was no sign of people— no debris, no soda cans or water bottles... and no packages."

"I didn't see anything, either." Felix chimed in.

"Serpico said the emails Lighter's assistant sent packages delivered to only one place on the island, that pineapple factory. If they're not there then—"

"It was a drop." Felix smiled at his deduction. "He picked them up."

Smoke wagged his hand. "Maybe he did. That is possible, but I think it's more likely someone else did."

Both David and Felix said, "Huh?"

"Lighter blew up an eighty-million-dollar plane to make everybody, including the FBI, believe he was dead. That deception gave him time to get set up on the island, stake out the hotel, and kidnap O. He also had to have anticipated, sooner or later, the FBI would crack his encrypted email and find his assistant. So, he had to be careful about getting what he needed on the island. The pineapple plant was a red herring serving two purposes. First it was a drop for the packages but it would also be a distraction, a false lead. With me so far?"

Both nodded.

"He had what he needed delivered and had somebody else pick up the packages. He is a one-man crew and he needed to stake out the hotel looking for the opportunity to grab O. That was the priority. I think he hired a kid to pick the stuff up."

David nodded but still looked unsatisfied. "Why a kid?"

"An adult would ask too many questions. A kid would only see the money."

So, he hires a kid who gets the packages but then what?"

"That's the question."

Smoke started pacing. "We have to put ourselves in his shoes. And the first thing we know for sure is, his options are limited. Since he came back from the dead, his face is everywhere and a description of the vehicle he used is in every cop car. He is forced to operate from wherever he is hiding. Logical?"

Felix and David nodded.

"So, he finds a kid, who is less likely to be keeping up with the news, and hires him to pick up his stuff."

"How would that work? The kid would have to have a car."

"Correct, the kid has to be older than sixteen, local and have access to a car."

David got on the logic bus. "Lighter gets a local kid, near where he is holding O, to drive and pick up the packages. He then returns to...?"

"The kid has to come back to get paid," Felix added.

David shakes his head. "Right, that too but where? Lighter meets this kid, some place, to pay him and get his stuff?"

"Not some place. The place." Smoke stops pacing. "I believe the kid will meet him within walking distance of where Lighter is holed up, deliver the packages, and get paid."

"Is the kid alive? I mean, Lighter killed the guys on the boat, his plane crew... everybody who saw him."

"I don't think so. A missing or dead kid will turn on a spotlight which he doesn't need. So, no, the kid is out there and we have to find him."

David's logic diminished. "Damn Smoke, I get what you're saying but even if you're right, I have to tell you, I'm a mathematical genius and I can't begin to calculate how high the odds are against finding that kid."

"Maybe, but I think our odds improve exponentially because we have Nalani Ka'ana'ana looking for him."

"Still, find one kid on an entire island? I don't know." David sounded unconvinced.

"We have narrowed the parameters considerably. A local kid got paid to deliver packages to a mysterious guy in a remote location."

Smoke leaned in close. "And, I can tell you for a fact, she will use all her powers to find that kid because she knows it will lead to the man who killed her granddaughter."

David nodded. "Got it, but Smoke, what do we do right now?"

Smoke sighed and leaned back to hold up the wall, again. "Nothing. We can't do a thing until we hear from Kiki."

Felix and David joined him against the wall.

Smoke sighed. "Come on Kiki, call."

His phone chimed.

Felix looked at his friend. "I wasn't before, but now I'm impressed."

Smoke pushed the accept button, put the phone to his

ear, listened, then pushed end. He started walking toward the exit, "Let's go."

Felix, following said, "Where?"

"Jurassic Park."

O tried to jump into the next wave but her feet were stuck in the sand. The water was colder than she expected, her body was shivering, and she could almost feel her lips turning blue. She could hear the waves getting closer and closer. It rose in front of her. It came crashing down. She couldn't breathe.

"No, no... not yet."

She felt hands under her arms, lifting her up.

Her toes felt the stool, not sand.

She coughed and gasped.

Reality entered her mind as air reentered her lungs.

When Lighter opened the door and saw her slumped over, feet still on the stool, the rope pulled tight on her neck, he hustled to prop her back up. He shook her awake then slowly drew his hands out from under her arms, half to make sure she could stand and half to feel her breasts.

Her face was white— her swollen eye angry red.

"That's better. I wouldn't want you crossing over to the other side before your time." He chuckled, "Actually, I should have said... before it is time." He looked at his watch. "Which is exactly three hours and twenty-seven minutes from now."

He twisted his wrist suddenly wondering how Patex Phillippe could turn nine ounces of platinum worth $22,000 into a $490,000 watch. He decided when he got to Bali, he would buy another and dissect it to discover why.

He flashed it in front of O's good eye. "Like it?"

O groaned, which caused her cracked lips to unstick.

"Oh my God, I have been a terrible host. You've been here all this time and I haven't offered you a drink. Where are my manners?"

Lighter sauntered out the door and returned carrying a bucket and a cup.

He could see her looking at the water splashing onto the floor.

Lighter stopped in front of her and took a cup of water from the bucket, then slowly drank it, watching her eye follow the water into his mouth.

"Ahhh. That was refreshing."

He dropped the cup, his face now taut. In one quick move, he gripped the bucket handle and threw the water in her face.

The force almost knocked her off the stool, but the water was cold and the shock of it tightened her muscles and stabilized her on the wobbly footstool.

Water poured from her hair and washed the dried blood from her head wound onto her face and blouse.

He stood back and admired his handiwork.

Her blouse was almost transparent and clinging to her body. "You always had great tits."

Her voice was weak and barely audible. "You have a little dick."

He stepped to her. His instant rage becoming a balled fist. He stepped forward and with all his weight behind his anger, struck her in her stomach.

She doubled over, collapsing lifeless onto his shoulders. He pushed her back and she slumped forward; her neck stretched by the rope. He walked quickly to the wall that held the rope's hook, loosened it, and let her sag to the floor. She was unconscious again which was unfortunate. His anger was delaying her demise.

He looked at his watch.

No time for this.

He picked up the bucket, refilled it, and dumped it on her head. Nothing.

"Fuck," he shouted.

He hated to revise a plan. Delays always led to mistakes, not to mention, they diminished the time he had to enjoy the moment.

She had to be fully awake when he relayed every detail of how he killed her sister. He wanted to see her spirit break when he told her it was her fault that her sister suffered because she had betrayed him to the FBI. He wanted to savor the moments when he used his knife to make her pay with excruciating pain for every year he was in prison.

She had to be awake. It wouldn't be any good for him if she passed out. She had to beg. All of them had—except the first one— the Hawaiian. He had gotten much better since then and he was going to break Olivia Bennet. Then and only then, would he end her.

He pulled a knife from a sheath on his belt, examining the thin blade but a thought distracted him.

I missed something.

He shook his head but that nagging thought returned.

What did I miss?

The knife point pricked his finger bringing him back into the game. A bubble of blood formed on his fingertip. He held it up and looked at it in the light. It was beautiful. A red balloon. Ready to burst.

25

Last day
The Final Hours

Smoke rode in the passenger seat, David in back, and Felix driving. No one was speaking. It was pre-game, locker-room, quiet.

"She'll be there." Felix spoke confidently.

Smoke sighed and turned to his friend. "I'm... I mean we... have to mount a stealth- assault without any recon and no plan."

Felix laughed. "You're kidding me, right?"

Smoke turned to stare out the window.

"Dude. I need you to listen to me." Felix's tone seemed angry.

Smoke didn't answer.

David tried to intervene. "Fel, I don't think he—."

Felix held up his hand. "I know you always have a plan. It's your thing. Plot the moves. Consider all the variables. Act in unison with your troops. But that can't happen here. Can it?"

Smoke remained silent.

"Well, can it?" Felix demanded an answer.

Smoke relented. "No, it can't happen this time."

"Correct, and do you remember the last time you didn't know what the lay of the land was or how many of the enemy you were facing?"

Smoke didn't answer.

"March 2, 2002, Afghanistan, the Shahi-Kot Valley, Operation Anaconda. We were pinned down, and I'm all shot to fuck. We had no support and no way out and you decide that wasn't the way it was going to go down."

Smoke grunted.

"You had no recon and no plan. You just acted. And, meanwhile, all by yourself you saved my life and the lives of fifty other grunts, just like me."

He turned to David. "He was awarded the Distinguished Service Medal, the highest medal the Army gives out."

"No shit?" David's voice had surprise and admiration.

"It should have been the Congressional, but no ranking officer witnessed it so he gets the silver. I'm still pissed."

"Okay, okay enough about that." Smoke didn't yell but he wanted the conversation to change direction.

Felix toned down. "Listen buddy, you saved me without a plan and no support. This time you have help." He put his hand on Smoke's shoulder. "We will save her. I know it in my soul."

Smoke rolled down the window letting the ocean supply music to fill his silence.

They were on Kamehameha Highway headed toward the tiny coastal village of Kaaaawa and Uncle Bobo's restaurant. There were only about 1,500 people living in the coastline community with almost no tourists. The ocean was shallow there, mostly reef and not surfer or swimmer friendly. All but a few residents were Hawaiian and everyone knew everyone.

"Look at that." David said in awe pointing to the mountain they were passing.

"That's the Kualoa Ranch. Remember the scene in Jurassic Park when the helicopter slowly dropped down the mountain and landed near the waterfall?"

"Great scene." Felix responded.

Smoke shared some local knowledge from his past. "It was filmed in that mountain range.

We're headed to where those mountains end at Makaua Park."

A few minutes passed and the SUV crossed over the two-lane road and pulled into a stone parking lot in front of a block, tropical-colored, building sporting two bright yellow beach umbrellas and a sign flaunting its famous smoked BBQ.

Kiki was waiting for them, leaning on his pick-up.

Smoke jumped from the truck. David and Felix followed.

Smoke wasted no time. "What do you have?"

"A boy who lives here was approached by Lighter to pick up packages at the pineapple plant. The boy was hesitant at first but Lighter gave him a hundred dollars and told him he would give him another hundred if he returned with all three packages, unopened."

"Great, that's a positive ID. Do you know where he is?"

Kiki put his hand on Smoke's shoulder and led him back across the highway, Felix and David in tow.

Kiki studied the mountain behind Uncle Bobo's, then pointed up. "Look about half way up the mountain, dead center in the middle and tell me what you see."

"I see it, there, a light." David pointed.

"Got it." Smoke nodded.

"What is it?" Felix asked.

"After Pearl Harbor, the US built artillery bunkers all over this island. Most were built on government property, but a couple were on private property. What you're looking at is a WWII bunker that was purchased by a tech millionaire a few years ago. He built a house around it but never moved in. He went bust and his fortress of solitude went unoccupied." Kiki turned to the trio. "Until Thursday."

Smoke breathed out, "Lighter."

"Has to be." Kiki smiled. "Nalani found the boy and him. She wants you to call her."

"I will, but first what do you know about the property?"

"Like every community along this highway, there are houses and commercial properties on every flat piece of ground available from water's edge to the base of the mountain. Back in off the highway, next to a couple of houses, is the access road built by the army. The tech guy built a big security gate. It has a camera. It'll be difficult to get up to the house undetected."

Smoke looked at Kiki. "But not impossible."

Kiki nodded. "For most."

"Sounds like a mission for a sneaky bastard."

Kiki smiled at his former Sergeant. "Hoorah."

Smoke looked up at the light on the mountain. "There has to be another way up there."

"Nalani said there is a back path leading to a tunnel and she's looking for more info."

"That it?" Smoke demanded.

Kiki scratched his head. "Maybe..." but he shook off the thought.

"What? There is something. What is it?"

"The bunker was built on a cliff. Nothing could grow because it is a steep slope. Climbing it would be dangerous in the daylight but at night, it would be—."

"Adventurous." Felix grinned.

"I was going to say suicidal." Kiki countered.

Smoke overruled objections and gave instructions. "Okay, here's the plan. Felix will go with Kiki—"

"No, I want to go with you."

Smoke shook his head. "Kiki needs a ladder to get over the gate. You're the tallest, so you're it."

Felix acted disappointed.

"David, are you good to go up with me?"

"Hoorah."

"We have," Smoke looked at his watch, "one hour fifty

minutes. Be careful, and quiet. If we are discovered..." He didn't finish because he could tell they understood.

The four walked across the road, side-by-side, down the quiet neighborhood road toward the driveway going up the mountain.

The view was spectacular. Lighter could see clear to the horizon, 180 degrees left and right. The original concrete wall he was leaning on was built in 1942, and only needed minor repair during the home building process. Back in the day, solid rock was excavated to house two long-range artillery guns. The opening where Lighter stood admiring the Pacific was where the barrels of two eight-inch cannons were positioned. It now was the balcony of a master bedroom. The tech man connected the bunker through a short tunnel leading to a plateau on the mountain where he built the rest of a magnificent house.

Lighter leaned over the edge and looked down into the darkness below. It was several hundred feet to the base. The first hundred feet was all of the rock that had been pushed out and dumped over the side— the rubble still preventing nature from reclaiming its rightful possession. The second hundred feet consisted of steep outcroppings of rock that protected his kingly perch.

He spit over the side, watching the phlegm fall.

I'll miss this place.

He pushed back from the wall, looked at his watch then

walked back to the house and the stairs down to where Dr. Olivia Bennet was going to die.

"The driveway begins at the end of the street." Kiki pointed as they walked.

There were houses close to the road and a dog began barking as they approached the last one.

"Okay," Smoke took command. "Kiki, how far up is the gate and what does it look like?"

"I reconned before you got here. The drive winds back though the brush to the gate. Its iron, tall, and built into the rock face. I could see a camera on the other side but I think I can disable it without being seen."

"Do you know the layout at the top?"

"Just from what I saw on Google Earth." Kiki bent to the ground and drew a floor plan in the dirt. "There's a house built around the old bunker— has to be living room, kitchen, bedrooms, the usual stuff. I think the garage is here and front door here." He looked up. "Most of the place is new but if it's like the rest of the bunkers on the island there will be caverns and tunnels that could lead anywhere inside the mountain."

Smoke stood up, then paced a little. "Lighter will be watching the driveway and front of the house. We know there's a camera at the gate but it's likely there will be more along the drive, either cameras or motion detectors." He stopped walking and faced his friends. "We also know there are two ways in, the front door, and through the balcony where we saw the light."

Smoke added the last detail. "Put your phones on vibrate. We'll coordinate when we get to the top." He paused and almost prayerfully said, "We have to take him by surprise otherwise… it won't be good." His voice returned to normal. "David and I will go in first. Either we'll get him or chase him out the door to Felix and Kiki. Ready?"

Four hands came together. "Hoorah."

Felix and Kiki started up the driveway.

Smoke and David pushed into the brush toward the mountain face.

The climb was difficult but not impossible. The handholds were small and footholds slippery, but they were making good time. David was ahead, with Smoke just a few feet behind. The crescent moon cast enough light to see but there was still a long shadow between them and the light coming from the balcony.

Smoke found a ledge sturdy enough to handle all his weight and he removed his hands from the wall, shaking out cramping fingers. "You okay?"

David gave a thumbs up sign. "Good."

Smoke looked up and as he did he saw a shadow moving. He immediately waved to David, getting his attention then pointed up.

A head poked over the railing and looked down.

Smoke's heart sank.

He'll see us.

They remained motionless.

The head scanned right and left then disappeared from view.

A minute went by, then Smoke motioned to start up again.

How did he not see us?

He moved up a few feet constantly looking up to the balcony.

Had to have been the shadow.

A cold wind hit him in the face. The weather to this point had been hot and he had sweated through his t-shirt.

Weird.

They were fifty feet from the balcony.

He grabbed a rock and pulled up. His handhold gave way and his foot slipped when his weight shifted. His other hand was locked onto a ledge of stone. He swung his free hand, that was dangling at his side, back to the wall. It was flat, nothing to grab.

There's no way I can hold on.

The cold wind hit him again. Somehow, he felt lighter. Gravity was supposed to be pulling him down. He was supposed to be falling to his death. But he wasn't.

He swung his body again, slapping the wall of rock in a different place. This time he found a crevice and his foot found an edge.

"You okay?" David whispered.

Smoke looked up. David had gotten up near the wall of the balcony.

Smoke nodded and started to climb, again.

What the fuck was that?

When Smoke got to the bottom of the balcony David pointed to an outcropping of rock. "If we can get up that ridge, we can get over the wall and onto the balcony."

"Okay, I'll be right behind you."

They shimmied up the face of the rock then one at a time, slipped down onto the concrete balcony. They crouched, heads darting back and forth, hoping they weren't detected.

The sound of the ocean suddenly getting louder told her Lighter would be coming through the door any second.

Buck up.

The pain in her shoulders, hands, legs, and neck had begun to throb in unison. Somehow, that made it easier to manage. She realized that maintaining her balance on the footstool was imperative and the key to her survival. Every time she lost her balance, the rope would tighten around her neck and the pain became unbearable.

When she heard the handle on the door turn, she wiggled her toes and gulped in courage.

"Well, well, I see the princess is still with us." Lighter marched into the room with a stride of superiority. "But I have to say, my dear doctor, you're looking worse for the wear."

He had changed clothes and was wearing blue jeans, a black t shirt. He carried a black hoody in his hand and hung it on the back of a metal chair. He pushed the chair with his foot closer to where O was hanging, then sat down, crossing his legs, relaxed and easy.

"I promised a bedtime story and I always keep my promises."

O shook her head, still wet from the bucket of water he dumped on her. Water flew in the air and landed on him.

"Hmmm... still defiant, I see." He brushed his pant leg. "So, a long time ago... I was in my apartment watching TV when the FBI burst through the door and escorted me off to Quantico. I was actually genuinely surprised when I found out you had chosen me to be the subject of a serial killer profile. I mean my girlfriend. A girl I chose because she reminded me of..." He stopped short and brushed his leg, again.

In spite of her current state, not finishing the sentence was the flaw that Dr. Olivia Bennet, the psychiatrist, was hoping to hear.

With an affected tone in his voice, he went on. "From many candidates I chose you specifically because you had been selected to intern by the special FBI unit charged with hunting down serial killers." He leaned forward a bit. "I was curious because I am a serial killer."

He glared at O, looking for the fear.

She didn't give it to him.

"I wanted to know how they worked and you were telling me everything I needed to know." His tone went dark again.

"Then, without telling me, you decided to do a profile on your boyfriend, me... as a class assignment. Then, out of nowhere, I'm dragged into FBI headquarters and interrogated."

O shifted her weight and tried to keep a steady gaze on him even though she had only one working eye.

"My lawyers got me out pretty fast but I was very, very mad." He put a finger to his lips in thought. "By the way, as a psychiatrist I'm sure you'll be interested to know that I have since determined that anger is a fatal flaw. So, I don't get mad anymore....I get even."

He stood up and walked up close. "But then...back then," he growled, "I got angry."

He started pacing back and forth. "I went right to your dorm and waited, getting madder and madder. Then there you were, walking like you hadn't a care in the world." He stopped and spoke slowly. "I came up from behind, put my hand over your mouth and a blade against your neck." His face leaned in close. "But... it wasn't you, was it?"

He backed off, his voice changing again, lighter almost whimsical. "Of course, I realized, it was your sister. And in that moment, somehow, and I don't completely understand it even now, I wasn't mad anymore."

He turned to her again. "What about that doc? Diagnosis?"

O tried to speak but nothing came out.

"What's that, didn't hear you." He put a hand to his ear, mocking her.

"Mommy."

He stood straight up, a stunned look on his face.

In spite of the pain, the hopelessness, the fear, he had inflicted on her, she knew that this moment would come. She knew in his moment of triumph; he would reveal his Achilles heel.

"I... you... no, no." His face became red. His hand raised—palm open.

"Mommy." Her voice was weak but the word was strong.

He halted in mid-slap—hand dropping to his side. He bent over and re-positioned the chair then sat, trying hard to put on a grin.

Her knees began to scream pain, but she fought it back.

"I... reminded you... of Mommy."

He coughed. "You were, back then, different."

"Mommy." She could barely get it out.

His eyes were wide and black. He leaned forward. "I killed...Mommy... in her sleep."

She didn't react, no sound, no grunt, no flicker in her eye.

He seemed disappointed. "She found out what I had been doing in my spare time. You must have found out about my... early work." He grinned. "I was just learning. Made a couple of small mistakes, one of which was allowing my mother to suspect that I was involved in the disappearance of a local wench." He whispered, "I was." He sighed and continued without passion. "She was so angry. Anyway, she told me she took dear old dad out of her will, and because of what I had done, she was going to leave everything to the ASPCA. I needed to act. So..." He uncrossed his legs and lowered his voice as if privacy was an issue. "Nicotinana tabacum, Nicotine. She was a chain smoker so no one bothered to do an autopsy, and even if they did a fatal dose is almost undetectable."

He studied her face looking for a reaction that she didn't give.

"She was asleep when I stuck her with the needle. Her eyes popped open and when she saw it who it was me. She stared in my eyes, scared at first but then her eyes turned mean."

He leaned back a little. "I laughed at her and she got scared again. Then I said, 'ASPCA.' and pushed the plunger."

"She... betrayed... you."

"Yes, she did, just like you. You betrayed me, and now you will die, just like her."

He stood, kicked over the chair, and reached for his knife and, as he did, his phone vibrated, violently.

He yanked it from his pocket and read the screen.

Activity on the driveway.

"Fuck."

He turned and ran for the door.

Somewhere within her desperation she felt a spark of hope.

Lighter glared at the computer screen marked GATE. There was no image, only snow. The second screen marked DRIVE was also blank. The third screen marked FRONT DOOR was operating, but showed no movement. Above the center screen was a black panel that had a drawing of the winding driveway from the gate to the front of the house. Small red lights had been drilled into the panel indicating where the motion detectors had been placed. The three on the lower portion of the drive were blinking.

Too soon. They're coming too soon.

Lighter examined his watch, calculating the time the intruders needed to reach the door. "Ten minutes to the door, another ten inside to find the basement."

I hate being rushed.

He left the room, trotting down the hall, running to help Olivia greet her maker.

Smoke heard someone running inside the house but from the balcony it was difficult to determine the origin. David and Smoke walked through the room to a door at the end of the short stone hallway. Smoke turned the handle slowly and peeked into a painted hallway.

He whispered to David, "I'll go right, you go left. Be careful. If he hears us coming, he'll kill her for certain."

David nodded and went out the door first.

Smoke went next moving carefully, staying close to the wall. There were three doors in front of him. He opened the first—a bedroom—good view, no furniture. He opened the second and saw the same. He went to the last door, opened it and saw the same empty room with a great view but he also saw a door, not a closet door, a metal door.

That's it.

He slowly, carefully, silently, turned the handle.

Lighter walked back into the chamber of horrors with his knife out and his face lit up with an ear-to-ear grin.

"Your heroes are here."

There was a slight glint of relief in her eye.

"Don't get too excited, Doctor. They're only halfway up the driveway and going slow, trying not to alert me to their presence. But, my darling, they are going to be too late. When they finally arrive... both of us will be gone. Me to an island vacation with a new identity and a new face and you... well... you're not going on vacation but you may need a new face."

Lighter pulled the rope to test the tension.

O's neck twisted sideways and the breath went out of her lungs.

He let go and she settled back onto the stool.

She mumbled something he couldn't hear.

Lighter cupped his hand behind his ear. "What's that? I couldn't hear you. Was that perhaps a plea for mercy?"

She mumbled again.

"See, I told you, sooner or later, everyone begs." He took a step closer. "Go on let's hear it, maybe this time I'll be so moved by your plea, I'll let you go." His grin was sardonic.

He took another step closer.

"I'm so..." her voice trailed off.

He turned his head, leaning his ear to her mouth.

O used every ounce of strength she possessed and cracked her head into his. "I'll tell your Mommy you said hi, shithead."

He wobbled away, holding his ear. "You fucking whore."

He pulled the knife from the scabbard and ran at her coming up from behind. He threw an arm around her chest and put the blade to her throat.

"Bye-bye, bitch."

"You're the bitch."

Smoke's words were cold and clear.

Lighter looked thunderstruck and almost dropped the blade.

No one spoke. No one breathed.

"Well..." Lighter stammered. "Look who it is. The bodyguard here to save the day."

"Drop the knife."

"No gun?" Lighter sized up his opponent. "No gun...no way."

"Walk...away."

"You move and I'll slice her ear to ear."

It took another moment for the next chess piece to move. "It will be the last thing you ever do." Smoke's voice was calm and strong.

O moaned in pain.

"I will fucking do it." Lighter was panicking and yelling. Sweat formed on his forehead and his eyes were darting back and forth.

"Drop the knife and walk away."

"Fuck both of you." Lighter dropped the knife so he could grab the leg on the stool with two hands. He yanked it out from under O, then ran for the door.

She dropped, the rope tightened, and her neck twisted sideways.

Smoke ran to her and lifted her up.

The rope slacked and she began choking.

Lighter hit the door running and Smoke could hear his footsteps going up the stairs.

"I got you," he whispered.

Smoke looked around. The hook was too far away. He looked up, saw the rope over the pipe, and jumped up grabbing the length of rope above her head. He swung his feet back and forth and pulled down. He could feel the pipe moving. Still holding her he dropped back to the floor.

"One more time."

He jumped again, this time the pipe broke in half and they fell—her on top of him. In seconds, he had her hands untied and her feet freed.

She could barely speak. Tears were pouring out and she sobbed from the deepest part of her soul.

"I got you." Smoke kissed her head, lifted her up, and carried her up the stairs.

Lighter stopped in the hall, listening. The commotion from the basement had attracted another set of feet. He heard them coming down the hall. He saw a weapon. A red fire extinguisher was set into a wall.

David was running toward the noise. When he came around a corner, he ran headfirst into Lighter's weapon and went lights out.

Lighter dropped the extinguisher and headed for his escape route.

Sooner or later Bitch, I'll get you. Nobody can protect you.

He went down the stair from the kitchen and through the garage. He opened the side door slowly and peeked out. It was quiet. Nothing was moving.

When the bunker was built, and because guns and ammo were never stored in the same place, a tunnel, used to store and move ammunition from the ground to the guns, was excavated. The entrance near the bunker had long since been covered with vegetation and was invisible unless one knew where to look. Lighter had found it and placed an emergency evacuation backpack inside containing cash, clothes, and passport. He just needed to cross a hundred feet, on the edge of the mountain, from the garage to the tunnel without being seen.

He scanned the area and bolted. He could hear his footsteps as they slapped against the rock.

He made it across to the thick growth of brush and vines at the mountain's edge. The sound of the waves roared up from the ocean below.

Lighter looked back to the house. Still no movement, then he began looking for the entrance to the tunnel.

The air suddenly got cold.

He was sweating and the cold wind chilled him to the bone. He felt heavy, barely able to move his hands. The cold air hit him again and he shivered against its force. He shoved his hands into the brush trying to locate the tunnel entrance. He probed again and again. The cold air pushed hard against him.

Smoke saw Lighter from the garage door and walked slowly toward him.

He came up on him from behind and touched Lighter on his shoulder.

Lighter, still trying to find the tunnel, let out a scream of surprise, and whipped around. He retreated putting a few feet of distance between him and Smoke. He was backing up, hand out, his head shaking back and forth.

"No. This isn't happening." Lighter shouted in disbelief. "Not to me. This can't be happening."

"It is and it's over."

Lighter continued backing up— one step, then another.

Smoke held up his hand. "Stop."

Lighter didn't. He stepped once more but the next one had no ground beneath it. His hands began failing wildly. He looked down and saw the ocean waves crashing into the rocks below.

Smoke reached out, grabbed his shirt, and held him there, half on this earth and half in the next world.

"Wait." Felix's voice bellowed as he and Kiki ran up to

the action. “I want to watch this bag of puss explode when he hits the rocks.”

“Noooo,” Lighter screamed.

Smoke held him there, just looking at him.

Lighter’s hands suddenly relaxed and dropped to his side. He was studying Smoke. “You won’t drop me. You can’t drop me. She wouldn’t want you to.”

Smoke jousted him.

Lighter gasped but then smiled.

“Drop this prick.” Felix said angrily.

Smoke turned to Felix. “Head to the house. Check on O. Make sure she’s okay.”

“But, I want to—.”

“David is with her but he was hurt.”

Felix took off with Kiki close behind.

When Smoke turned to Lighter, he saw he was wearing a small smile of confidence.

“As much as I like this view, I think you should pull me back. I know you’re not going to drop me.”

Another voice was heard.

“You’re wrong. He could drop you and sleep like a baby.” Nalani Ka’ana’anaa emerged from the brush.

“Who the fuck is this old woman?” Lighter said, now looking at the tiny Hawaiian woman.

Smoke pulled Lighter back to solid ground.

A voice came from behind the royal grandmother of Hawaii.

“She be the grandmama of my sista. Me name is Makana. You bemember my twin sista, don’t you?”

When Lighter saw the younger woman come out from behind Nalani, his attitude changed. "Ah...Umm, I mean, no, I don't know what you're talking about."

Smoke pulled Lighter close. His face was inches away from his.

Lighter was a sack of helpless. His shoulders were slumped and his face white.

"There's someone else here who is going to help you remember Makana's sister."

The big man who had been at the shrine and had accompanied the grandmother to the hotel stepped out of the tunnel.

Smoke looked Lighter in the eye. "This is Ezekiel. The woman you called old is his mother." He grabbed Lighter's shirt and lifted him to his toes then pointed to the girl whose face was as fixed as stone. "Wahini means beautiful young girl. Ezekiel is the father of this wahini, and her name is Makana. Her sister... her twin sister, was Kalani. She was the wahini you kidnapped and killed eighteen months ago."

He dropped Lighter back to the ground then spun him around and sent him careening to Ezekiel.

Lighter screamed when a giant hand, vice-gripped his shoulder.

Nalani Ka'ana'anaa took Smoke's arm. "Did you call on the Sisters of Kauai for help?"

Smoke sputtered, "No... not really," but his mind raced back to almost falling from the cliff. "But something happened that I can't explain. I almost died getting here."

Nalani smiled, "Did you feel a cold wind?"

"Yes, I did." Smoke's face registered a bit of surprise.

Nalani beckoned him to lean down.

He complied and she kissed his cheek. "You didn't have to call on the Magic Sisters, I did it for you."

She beckoned to Makana and together they walked through the brush and into the tunnel.

Ezekiel followed them, Lighter in front. He was helpless and in the grip of a man no fortune could buy.

Lighter's screams echoed off the walls, gradually diminishing, till they disappeared forever.

O was sitting up, back against the wall. Felix and Kiki were now unnecessarily standing guard.

"Did you all see what happened over there?"

"We did." Kiki answered. "It was a reckoning, a settling of accounts. It's an ancient Hawaiian tradition called Kaulike—like, putting things back in balance, ho'okaulike —tribal justice."

"You have any problems with that?"

O turned to look up at him with her good eye. "With what?"

"What I did...I gave him to—."

O stopped him with a mere brush of her hand.

"Felix, would you and Kiki take David into the kitchen and see if you can round up some ice for David's head and get some for O's eye too, please."

Felix stammered, "Shit, of course. Geeze sometimes, I

just don't think."

Smoke smiled. "Sometimes?"

Felix gathered up his mate and they went off to complete the errand.

O looked up at him. "I cannot imagine what I look like."

"How about beautiful?"

"Right," she scoffed.

Smoke plopped down beside her. He lowered his head, suddenly exhausted.

She put her hand over his. "Smoke...my love... can we please, go home now?"

Smoke blew a long deep breath into the warm tropic air.

"App - so - fucking - lootly."

ALSO BY PAUL EBERZ

SMOKE: A White Collar Crime

"...thrilling, absorbing...and very well written. Intriguing plot (is) well-conceived and developed... suspenseful... The work is very well-structured allowing the story to build suspense progressively, leaving the reader hungry to continue reading." Devon LaBonte Austin McCauley Publishers, London, New York, Sharjah.

ABOUT THE AUTHOR

Paul Eberz authored *Reckoning* as the second book in a trilogy. The first was *Smoke - White Collar Crime* and the final book is expected to be ready for publication in 2022. In addition to this series, Eberz is preparing two additional novels, a historical fiction mystery about the death of JFK and a *Call of the Wild* adventure story set in 1849.

Eberz recently retired from the construction industry where he held executive positions in Fortune 500 companies and traveled the country working with Native Americans. Born in Philadelphia, he now resides in Florida and New Jersey.

www.ingramcontent.com/pod-product-compliance
Lightning Source LLC
Chambersburg PA
CBHW070543310726
48982CB00010B/1464/J
* 9 7 8 1 7 3 5 2 5 6 6 3 4 *